"I'm sorry about last night."

She glanced at Jesse, and knew instantly he was talking about the kiss. Her pulse quickened and her mouth felt dry.

"It's me who should be apologizing," June said. "For locking you up. But I had to be sure that you weren't the mole who'd brought the henchmen so close last night."

June looked up at him and her heart kicked.

"You're the reason they came looking, Jesse. Samuel is after your blood. I'm really sorry I locked you up."

Jesse's gaze went to the door.

"It's not locked. You're free to go."

He took a step toward her. June's knees felt weak.

"June, I am sorry, about the kiss"

"I'm not," she said, very quietly, her cheeks warming.

Dear Reader,

I love stories about second chances. We all make mistakes. Sometimes the results of those mistakes can be devastating, leaving us trapped by feelings of guilt that dog us through the remainder of our lives.

But what if, as in a fairy tale, a wand could be waved and a wish granted that enabled us to forget, just for a while, the guilt and pain that traps us in the past and stops us from truly living and moving forward into the future?

In romance, amnesia is often the magic wand that grants our characters that second chance. This is what happens to my hero in *The Perfect Outsider* when an accident temporarily steals his memory. But when my heroine, a rescuer at heart, tries to save him, it's he who saves her instead. By being forced to live solely in the present, he shows her how to forgive herself, and how to live again.

I hope you enjoy June and Jesse's journey toward their second chance at love.

Loreth Anne White

Watch out for these titles in the Perfect, Wyoming miniseries:

Special Agent's Perfect Cover by Marie Ferrarella—January 2012

Rancher's Perfect Baby Rescue by Linda Conrad—February 2012

A Daughter's Perfect Secret by Kimberly Van Meter—March 2012

Lawman's Perfect Surrender by Jennifer Morey—April 2012

Mercenary's Perfect Mission by Carla Cassidy—June 2012

LORETH ANNE WHITE

The Perfect Outsider

ROMANTIC
SUSPENSE

Special thanks and acknowledgment to
Loreth Anne White for her contribution to the Perfect,
Wyoming miniseries.

Recycling programs
for this product may
not exist in your area.

ISBN-13: 978-0-373-27774-2

THE PERFECT OUTSIDER

www.Harlequin.com

Printed in U.S.A.

Books by Loreth Anne White

Other titles by this author available
in ebook format.

LORETH ANNE WHITE

was born and raised in southern Africa, but now lives in Whistler, a ski resort in the moody British Columbian Coast Mountain range. It's a place of vast wilderness, larger-than-life characters, epic adventure and romance—the perfect place to escape reality. It's no wonder she was inspired to abandon a sixteen-year career as a journalist to escape into a world of romantic fiction filled with dangerous men and adventurous women.

When she's not writing you will find her long-distance running, biking or skiing on the trails and generally trying to avoid the bears—albeit not very successfully. She calls this work, because it's when the best ideas come.

For a peek into her world visit her website, www.lorethannewhite.com. She'd love to hear from you.

To editors Patience Bloom, Keyren Gerlach and Shana Smith. And to fellow authors Marie Ferarella, Linda Conrad, Kim Van Meter, Jennifer Morey and Carla Cassidy—for making this series happen. It's been a pleasure to work with you all.

Chapter 1

Eager was trained to alert on human scent.

And that's exactly what his handler, June Farrow, was hoping to find as she worked her four-year-old black Lab in a zigzag pattern across the wind, the glow from her headlamp casting a pale beam into blackness. It was 4:00 a.m. Cold. The cloud cover was low, and rain lashed down through trees.

As June and her K9 worked their way up the thickly forested slope, the terrain grew treacherous, with steep gullies and hidden caves. June prayed that Lacy Matthews and her three-year-old twins, Bekka and Abby, were holed up in one of those caves, dry and safe from the storm.

Safe from Samuel Grayson's men.

Because if Samuel's men had found them, they were as good as dead.

Swaths of mist rolled down from the peaks and June's hiking boots began to lose traction. More than once she had to grab onto brambles to stop from slipping down into one of the ravines hidden by the darkness and bush. Sweat prickled under her rain jacket and moisture misted her safety glasses. Water ran in a stream from the bill of her hat and it trickled uncomfortably down her neck.

While Eager was able to barrel like a tank through the increasingly dense scrub, the twigs began to tear at June's clothes, hooking into her hair, clawing at her backpack, slowing her progress. This, she thought, as she stilled a moment to catch her breath, was why search-and-rescue teams used dogs—they could access places with ease that humans could not, especially a dog like Eager, who, with his stocky, deep-chested frame and thick coat, was impervious to the claw of brambles. And, having been bred from gundog stock, he was able to remain calm in the presence of loud rescue choppers and the big excavation machines often present in urban rescue.

June listened carefully to her surroundings, hoping to catch the faint sound of a woman's cry on the wind. But a forest was never quiet, and in a storm like this, trees talked and groaned and squeaked as their trunks and branches rubbed together in the wind. Pine cones and broken branches bombed to the ground, and rain plopped from leaves. The pine needles in the canopy above swished with the sound of a river.

She could detect no cry for help amid the other sounds of the stormy night.

Tension coiled tight in her stomach.

Working solo was foolish, particularly for an experienced SAR tracker who knew better. But a desperation to find those three-year-old twins and their mother burned like fire in June's chest, outweighing all caution.

Her own son had been three when he'd died.

If June had managed to dig deeper into her own reserves, search harder, faster, sooner, all those years ago, she might have arrived in time to save Aiden. Now she *had* to save Bekka and Abby. The reason they were lost in the woods was partly June's fault, and they'd been missing for two nights now. The clock was ticking and guilt weighed heavy.

"Eager!" she yelled over the wind. "Go that way, boy!"

Eager more sensed than saw his handler's directional signal, and he veered in an easterly direction, moving across the base of glistening-wet rock. All June could see of him was the pale green glow of his LED collar, and every now and then the wet reflection of his coat as he cut across the beam of her headlamp.

The moisture was actually working in Eager's favor—it enhanced his scenting abilities, but the wind was confounding. It punched down through holes in the canopy and swirled in eddies around the forest floor, carrying any scent that might have been pooling on the ground or in gullies with it.

June saw her dog hesitate a moment, then suddenly the green collar bobbed as Eager went crashing off in a new direction across the flank of a cliff.

He had scent.

June rushed after him, heart pounding as she shouldered through bushes and skidded over wet deadfall. Then she lost sight of the fluorescent light. She stilled, catching her breath as she wiped rainwater from her face. Her hand was shaking, and June realized she was exhausted.

She was going to make a fatal error like this.

She willed herself to calm. Life depended on it, and not just hers.

But as she dug deep for self-control an image hit her hard and suddenly of a search gone wrong five years ago. A search that resulted in the dramatic deaths of her husband and son. She closed her eyes for a moment, trying to shake the accompanying and familiar sense of sheer and utter desperation.

It had happened because of a cult.

Her husband, Matt, had been sucked in by a religious organization, and when June had pressured Matt to leave, he'd kidnapped Aiden from day care, planning to take him to live on the cult compound.

Thunder crashed and grumbled in the mountains and another gust of wind swished through the trees. June's nerves jumped. She braced her hand against the trunk of a tree.

Focus. You're doing this for them. Everything you do now is because you messed up that time.

That devastating incident was why she now worked for EXIT, a national organization quietly dedicated to aiding victims of cults. June's life mission had become running halfway houses for cult members who wanted to "escape." If she could rescue others, if she could get them into safe houses where they could access exit-counseling, it might give meaning, somehow, to the gaping maw of loss in her own life.

It might help assuage her guilt for not having understood how to help Matt back then.

And it was because of Samuel Grayson and his dangerous cult of Devotees that June was in Cold Plains, Wyoming, now. She'd arrived on behalf of EXIT three months ago. Right now she had five Devotees in the safe house. Lacy and her children were supposed to make the number eight.

But something had gone wrong—Lacy and her girls had failed to meet June at a designated meeting place in the woods on Monday evening, from where June was to have escorted them to the secret safe house.

June had searched the area, tracking Lacy and her twins back along the trail that led down the mountain toward the town. Around 11:00 p.m. that night, Eager had alerted on a small, sparkly red shoe belonging to one of the twins. The shoe had been lying just off the trail. From that point the footprints had gone into the forest. June and Eager had followed Lacy's trail deeper into the woods where more footprints appeared, and it looked as though two men had started following Lacy and the twins. June put Eager on the tracks, but the storm had broken and they'd lost the scent.

Before heading back to the safe house to grab an hour or two of rest that night, June had first hiked over to the southeastern flank of the mountain where she dropped the red shoe as a decoy. She knew Cold Plains Police Chief Bo Fargo would be mounting a search party and calling for SAR volunteers as soon as Lacy was reported missing, and she didn't want the official SAR party anywhere near the safe house or the area where Lacy had actually vanished.

Chief Fargo was bad news. He was a Devotee and one of Samuel's main men. June needed to find Lacy and the girls before the cops did, or they'd end up right back in Samuel's clutches.

On Tuesday morning when Lacy had failed to open up her coffee shop, she and her children were reported missing. By Tuesday afternoon, Chief Fargo had called in SAR volunteers and a search had been mounted. Fargo had asked June to see if she and her K9 could track any scent from Lacy's house.

By Tuesday evening, June and Eager had led the search crew to the decoy shoe on the east flank. A command center had been immediately set up on the flank of the mountain and the area divided into grids. Teams had searched until dark, volunteers agreeing to regroup at first light Wednesday.

Instead of grabbing a few hours' rest like the others, June and Eager had hiked straight back to the west flank, where they were now in the dark predawn hours of a stormy Wednesday morning. And, as the hours ticked by, June was beginning to fear the worst.

Suddenly, Eager started barking excitedly somewhere in the dark. Energy punched through June.

He'd found something!

She clambered up the slope into blackness, making for

the sound of his barking. Rain beat down on her, branches snapped back against her glasses. She felt pain as something cut across her face, but she kept moving, faster. Then she heard her dog come crashing back through the woods in her direction.

He leaped up against her, his breath warm against her face, and he barked again before spinning around and bounding back to his find.

"Where is it, Eager? *Show me, boy!*"

June reached him standing over something in tight scrub under the cliff face. She crouched down, and with the back of her hand she edged aside dripping leaves. And there, in the halo of her headlamp, was a handgun in black loam.

Tension rippled through June.

"Good boy, Eager!" She tried to pump enthusiasm into her praise as she pulled out his bite toy and began a rough game of tug, rewarding him for his success before anything else. Eager lived for his tug game and June's praise. It was what kept him focused for hours at a time on a search.

She let him yank his toy out of her grip. "You win, boy. You got it!"

He clamped his jaws over the bite toy and shook it wildly, mock-killing it, then he gamboled around like a puppy, as goofy in his big Labrador heart as he'd always be. While he played, June turned her attention to the weapon.

In her line of work articles found on a search could become evidence in a crime, so she was careful to preserve any prints as best she could in an environment like this, with no equipment. At the same time she knew that handing this weapon over to Chief Fargo would be as effective as throwing it into a black hole. The FBI, however, might want to see this. Special Agent Hawk Bledsoe had been watching this town for some time, and his noose was slowly closing around Samuel.

June shrugged out of her backpack and located her digital camera. She snapped several pictures of the gun—a Beretta—then recorded the location of her find on her GPS.

Using her bandanna to pick the weapon up, she aimed the muzzle to the ground, released the clip. Three rounds remained inside the eleven-round magazine. She racked back the slide, popping another round out of the gun chamber. Once she was certain it was unloaded, she wrapped it in her bandanna and secured it at the bottom of her backpack.

June carried her own handgun in a holster on her hip tonight.

Anxiety whispered through her as Eager brought his toy back, snuffling like a happy pig. June took it from him, told him to be quiet. She listened intently to the forest, and an eerie sense of a presence nearby rolled over June. With it came a sharp stab of vulnerability.

She and her dog were in the dark, surrounded by miles of Wyoming wilderness, and even if she wanted to call for help, there was no cell reception on this side of the mountain. June's sole backup was a two-way radio connection to the safe house in the next valley. Even so, the current occupants of the safe house were ill-equipped to help her out of a pickle. And the radios were for serious emergency calls only—there remained the possibility that Samuel's henchmen could be in the area and pick up a broadcast should they manage to tune in to the same frequency.

Inhaling deeply, June got up from her haunches. She took hold of her dog's collar, which made him look up into the glow of her headlamp, his eyes reflecting the light like a zombie beast.

"Eager, are you *ready?*" she whispered. "You want *work,* boy?"

His muscles quivered as he waited for the release.

She let go of his collar, swinging her arm out in the direction she wanted him to work. *"Search!"*

And off he went sniffing the air, left to right. She followed, fighting down fatigue and despair as the first gray light of dawn fingered through the leaves and rain.

Eager suddenly got wind of fresh human scent, and his head popped sharply in a ninety-degree angle to the left. His tail wagged loosely as he zeroed in on the scent cone.

"Not too far, Eager!" June yelled, trying to keep up, but suddenly he vanished.

She stopped in her tracks, breathing hard, heart hammering. Then she heard the crash of breaking brush, followed by wild barking. Quickly, she scrambled in the direction of the barking, but as she pushed through low scrub, the ground suddenly gave out under her and she realized too late that she'd overshot the lip of a ravine hidden by a tangle of brambles. Groping wildly for purchase, June tumbled down a steep bank.

Her fall was halted as her shoulder *whumped* into a log. She gasped in pain and lay still for a moment, mentally regrouping as sweat and rain dribbled into her eyes. Tentatively she edged onto her side and with relief she realized she wasn't badly hurt, just bruised. She kicked the toes of her boots into the loam on the steep slope to find purchase, and she began to inch down to the ravine floor. Eager came gamboling and crashing back up the slope, oblivious to the precariousness of her situation, and he hit her body with his front paws, as if to say, *"Come, come, I found it, Mom, I found it!"*

"Good boy—take it easy," she said a little shakily. "I'm right behind you, buddy."

It was dark at the base of the bramble-choked gulley as June pushed branches aside and saw what Eager had found.

A man lay on his side. Big. Maybe six foot two. His face was hidden from view and his dark hair glistened with rain. His denim jacket and jeans were soaked through. June noted he wore serious hiking boots, and the bottom of his left pant leg was soaked in what looked like blood.

"Good boy, Eager," she whispered, tossing his toy to the side for him to play with as she crouched down beside the man.

June carefully rolled him over. His head flopped back, exposing a mean gash across his temple. She felt his carotid. He was alive, but unconscious, his skin cold.

Her peripheral thought was that he was devastatingly good-looking, in a rough, tanned, mountain-man kind of way, and maybe in his early thirties. She hadn't seen him around Cold Plains before—a guy like this would be hard to miss.

Then she caught sight of the leather holster at his hip— empty. And for a nanosecond June froze. It must have been his Beretta she'd found.

Had he fired at Lacy and her children?

Sweat broke out over her body and her paramedic training warred with a need for safety. Because if this man was carrying, he could very likely be one of Samuel's henchmen.

Samuel eschewed weapons in the hands of his Devotees, but his personal murderous militia were the exception.

Bitterness filled her mouth as she reached quickly for his leather belt, first removing a GPS handheld device so she could undo his buckle, which was engraved with the name *Jesse*. It sounded like a brand of Western wear. June quickly undid the buckle and the zipper of his jeans. She edged his pants down over his hip. And there it was—a small *D* tattoo—the branding mark Samuel Grayson personally gave each one of his true Devotees. And if this Devotee was carrying—he was most certainly a henchman.

Bastard.

But before she could think through her next move, the man's eyes flared open and he grabbed her wrists. A hatchet of panic struck into her heart. She tried to jerk free, but his grip was like iron.

He blinked into the glow of her headlamp, and June saw his eyes were a deep and unusual shade of indigo-blue. In them she could read confusion.

"What are doing with my pants?" His voice came out hoarse, rough. Eager growled, hackles rising.

"Quiet, Eager," June whispered, fighting to tamp down the fear swelling inside her. "I'm here to help you," she said as calmly as she could. "I...needed to see if you had the Devotee tattoo on your hip—to see if you were a local, one of us, from Cold Plains."

Confusion filtered deeper into his eyes. "Devotee?" he said.

"You have a *D* tattooed on your hip, the one Samuel Grayson personally gives his true followers," she said.

He stared at her, features blank. Then he tried to move his head, wincing as he did. The movement caused fresh blood to flow from the gash down the side of his face. His jaw was dark with stubble. She wondered how long he'd been lying here.

"Where am I?"

"Looks like you took a tumble into the ravine," she said. "You've got a pretty nasty cut on your head and your leg is bleeding. Let me go so I can look at it."

He stared at her, refusing to relinquish his viselike grip on her wrists. His hands were big, calloused. He was impossibly strong, even in his injured state.

June's mouth went dry. She could easily disappear down here with her dog, and no one would find her until it was too late.

"I haven't seen you around Cold Plains," she said as calmly as she could. "My name is June Farrow. I'm a part-time paramedic with the Cold Plains Urgent Care Center, and a SAR volunteer. This is Eager, my K9. He's pretty friendly, but if he thinks you're going to hurt me, he'll attack. I'd hate for that to happen, so why don't you let go of me and maybe I can help you?"

His gaze shifted to her dog. Slowly he let go of her hands.

June lurched up to her feet, jumped back and pulled out her gun. She aimed it at his head.

Careful, don't blow your cover, June.

To the best of her knowledge, no one in town knew she worked against Samuel. Like most of the two thousand residents of Cold Plains, June attended his motivational seminars on Being the Best You. She pretended to hang on to his every word, painting herself as a potential Devotee on the cusp of conversion. Samuel had even suggested she come to one of his private counseling sessions, which were where he did most of his mind control. He was a master at preying on any insecurity, exposing a person's deepest fears and then promising to make them feel safe. His message was that as long as you were a Devotee, you were safe—in turn he wanted obedience, time and money. But if you tried to escape, as Lacy just had, he wanted you dead.

"What's your name?" she demanded. "What are you doing out here in the woods?"

His hand went to the holster at his hip.

"I have your weapon. It's missing rounds. Did you shoot at them?"

He frowned.

"Shoot at who?"

"There's a young mother and her two children lost in these woods. I'm looking for them. Are you chasing them? Did you hurt them?"

He tried to sit up, groaning in pain. And as he moved June caught sight of something lying in the soil behind his shoulder—*a little, sparkly red shoe.*

Rage arrowed through her body, obliterating any trace of fear.

"Don't move! Or I will shoot you dead. Where did you find that shoe?"

"I don't know what you're talking about... I can't seem to remember...anything." His voice faded and he touched the wound on his brow, his fingertips coming away bloody. He stared at the blood, a look of disorientation on his rugged features.

"What's your name?" she repeated.

His gaze lifted slowly and met hers, and in his eyes June saw the beginnings of fear. "I... Jesus—I don't know my name," he whispered.

June swallowed.

Was he playing her?

What was she going to do with him now? Leave him out here to die—which he might if he was disoriented and lost more blood. And if hypothermia kicked in, he was finished.

June glanced at his GPS device lying near her feet.

"Where were you going when you fell down here?"

"I told you, I don't know."

"Which way is Cold Plains?" she said.

"Cold Plains?"

"You've never heard of Cold Plains?"

"I..." He cursed softly.

June swore to herself. She was not capable of leaving him to die out here. She was programmed to rescue, had been ever since she was a kid. June was the child who saved bugs from puddles. It was why she became a paramedic. It was why she worked for SAR—she was wired to help those in despair.

But she had not been able to help her husband. The sudden memory stab, the sharp reminder of her inadequacies, hurt.

Holding her gun on him with one hand, she reached down and picked up his GPS with the other. She pressed the menu button, saw that he'd been saving his route—and he appeared to have hiked in not from Cold Plains, but from over the mountains.

"You've come a long way," she said. "You've saved a route into these mountains from forty miles north—where were you before that?"

He groaned, lay back. "I wish I knew."

He needed help—he was still losing blood. He might have been lying here for hours. She had no idea how bad his leg wound was. And daylight was beginning to filter down into the ravine. She had maybe an hour to hike all the way down into Cold Plains and to head around to the search base camp on the other side of the mountain, and she'd still found no sign of Lacy and the twins.

Her only solution—if one could even call it that—was to take this stranger back to the safe house and hold him there until she could fetch FBI Agent Hawk Bledsoe. It was risky, but she didn't have time to think further.

"I'm going to help you, okay?"

He nodded.

"I'm putting this gun away." *Please don't let this be a mistake*... "And if you hurt me, you're going to die out here, alone, understand?"

His eyes remained locked onto hers. "I don't hurt people."

She holstered her Glock. "How would you know?" She shrugged out of her backpack as she spoke. "You don't even know your name."

Crouching down next to him, she opened her pack and removed her first-aid kit. His pulse was within range, and he was breathing okay—she'd seen that much.

"Can you move your limbs? Any numbness in your extremities?"

He grunted. "No. Just...weak."

Blood loss was her priority now.

"I'm going to cut open the bottom of your jeans. I want to take a look at that injury on your leg," she said as she reached for her scissors and began splitting open the base of his pants. The gash on his head was bad, but the one on his leg could be worse—she needed to see what she was dealing with.

He groaned in pain as she peeled the bloodied and rain-soaked denim off a deep gash on his calf.

He was going to need sutures.

She worked quickly to clean and dry the wound as best she could, shielding him from the rain with her body. There was no arterial damage or obvious fracture—just a big surface gash probably caused by sharp rock during his fall.

Pulling the edges of the cut together, she applied butterfly sutures from her kit. Then she wound a bandage tightly around his calf, urgency powering her movements.

"This should work as a temporary stopgap," she said as she began to clean the cut on his temple.

His gaze caught hers and she stilled for a second—the intensity in his eyes was disturbing. He smelled faintly of wood smoke.

"You been camping?" she said.

He inhaled sharply as disinfectant touched his cut. "I—I really don't know." Then, as he thought deeper: "Do I have a backpack with me?"

"I can't see one."

He closed his eyes, clearly straining to remember. Then he swore softly again. "I feel as if I might have had a pack or something. That I was going somewhere...important."

The cut on his head, if ugly, was also superficial. However, given his apparent memory loss, he could be suffering from some sort of intracranial hemorrhaging due to blunt-force trauma, which could become dangerous.

"I'm going to give you three words," she said. "*Radio, belt,*

Jesse. Can you memorize them for me? I'm going to ask you to repeat them to me in a little while, okay?"

"Radio, belt, Jesse," he repeated. "Got it."

His voice was beautiful, she thought, deep and husky like Matt's used to be. Matt had been fair, but similar in stature to this man—an ace helicopter pilot she'd met on one of her very first recue missions. She'd loved going camping with Matt—loved the way fire smoke lingered in his checked lumberjack shirt, how the stubble on his cheeks grew rough in the wilderness. Emotion pricked into her eyes. June pushed it away, startled at the freshness of it all. It had been five years. She'd dealt with it.

"You sure you don't recall firing your weapon?" she said, trying another angle as she taped more butterfly sutures to the cut on his temple. Eager was watching obediently from the side, waiting for new directions.

"No."

"But you knew you had a gun—you went for it at your hip."

"I…guess."

"And you're sure you didn't see a young mother and her children in the woods?"

"No!" Frustration bit into his tone "I'm not the hell sure of *anything.*"

He was scared of what was happening to him, thought June.

"Why do you have that little red shoe?"

He was quiet a moment, then his eyes flickered as if a memory suddenly crossed before them. "I told you, I have no idea what you're talking about."

June wondered if he was lying.

"That shoe—" she jerked her chin to where it lay "—belongs to a three-year-old twin. She and her sister call them their Dorothy shoes. They like to take them everywhere so they can put them on and click their heels like Dorothy in *The Wizard of Oz* and be home safe whenever they need to be. Their names are Rebecca and Abigail. Their mother is Lacy Matthews. Lacy runs the coffee shop in town. They've been missing in these woods for two nights, and I'm thinking the girls will be wanting their magic shoes to take them home about now."

His gaze went to the shoe and he stared at it as if he'd never seen it before in his life.

"There, that should tide you over," she said as she applied a bandage over the sutures.

He pulled up his jeans zipper, buckled his belt and immediately tried to get to his feet, but he swayed and slumped heavily back to the ground.

"Easy, big guy," she said, helping him back up by the arm. "You lost a fair bit of blood. Move too fast and you're going down like a rock."

"I need to go—" He started to stumble through the brush, then swayed and leaned heavily on her. "I've got to get to…" His voice faded, and his features twisted in frustration.

"Get to where?" she said.

"I… Jesus, *I don't know.* I was going somewhere. Urgent—had to do something…important, for someone. Something…dangerous."

A chill trickled down her spine.

"Do something for whom? Samuel Grayson?"

"I… The name feels familiar."

"Yeah," she said bitterly. "He'd be the one who tattooed your hip. Can you walk, if you lean on me like this?" She hooked his big arm around her neck, taking the brunt of his weight across her shoulders.

June began to help him up the bank. He was solid muscle and their progress was slow. When the bank got too steep, she let him climb in front of her while she supported him from behind. She also wanted to be in a position where she could draw her gun again if she had to.

June's immediate goal was to get this injured stranger into the safe house, further assess his condition and administer whatever additional medical aid she could. Then she was going to press him hard on the whereabouts of Lacy and the twins—he was her *only* clue right now.

She'd also ask the others in the house if they'd seen him around Cold Plains. If they did recognize the stranger as one of Samuel's cult enforcers, she'd keep him under lock and key, fetch Hawk Bledsoe and hand him over to the FBI.

Hawk was one of the few people June could totally trust in this surreal, picture-perfect and sick little town. Four months ago Hawk's sister-in-law, Mia, had been brought to an EXIT psychologist for "deprogramming," which is how EXIT had got wind of the cult in Cold Plains.

Mia had told EXIT there were other members who wanted to get out, but they had no resources and were afraid for their lives if they spoke out against Samuel. Mia had passed on the name of Hannah Mendes, a widow in her seventies with a ranch on the outskirts of Cold Plains. Hannah had been trying to set up a safe halfway house with the aid of her sister-in-law from Little Gulch over in the next valley. EXIT had contacted June and asked if she'd run the house and help Hannah with an evacuation program. They presently had five people in the safe house waiting to move into an EXIT program, and June had done the early stages of counseling with them. Lacy and her twins would have brought the number of occupants to eight.

As they edged up over the ravine lip, rain was coming down hard again and the wind soughed, swirling mist like wraiths through the trees. Dawn had done little to dissipate the gloomy eeriness of the forest. June paused and gave the stranger some water. His face had a pallor that worried her, and he was weakening.

"Where are we going?" he said, handing her water bottle back to her.

"Shelter. A safe place." Hooking his arm over her neck again, supporting his weight with her shoulders, June led him through the trees toward a hidden crevasse that would lead into caves and a tunnel to Hidden Valley on the other side of the mountain. That's where the safe house was.

As he began to lean more heavily on her, June prayed she wasn't taking a cult enforcer, her worst kind of enemy, into the very heart of their safe house.

Chapter 2

As they neared the opening of the crevasse that led to the cave tunnel, the pager on June's hip sounded. Tension whipped through her. She leaned her shoulder against the rock face, the stranger heavy against her body as she checked the page.

Chief Fargo.

Her pulse quickened. The police chief was probably wondering why she and Eager hadn't shown up with the rest of the SAR team at first light this morning. June would never make it down there in time now, not if she had to take this injured man back to the safe house first. Sweat prickled over her lip.

With the FBI's noose tightening around Samuel, and with more and more of his Devotees disappearing into some rumored safe house, the entire town was on edge, looking for the traitor among them. The *last* thing June needed was to give Fargo, Samuel or anyone else in Cold Plains cause to suspect her.

As part of her of her cover, June rented an outbuilding on Hannah Mendes's ranch as her "official" residence in Cold Plains while she worked two days a week as a paramedic for the urgent-care ambulance service.

Hannah covered for June on all the other nights and days she spent working at the cave house in the mountains. The ranch was likely the first place Fargo might go looking for June when she didn't show up for the search party or answer this page. Fargo might see June's truck still in the driveway, start asking questions. Hannah could come under scrutiny, as well.

June cursed to herself—she was going to need a damn fine explanation to satisfy Fargo.

This community with its seemingly picture-perfect facade was like a ticking time bomb. June just wished the FBI would hurry up and get something they could actually use to take Samuel down and prosecute him before the whole place blew sky-high, Waco-style.

She hooked her pager back onto her belt and tried to get her patient moving again, but his legs were buckling under him and he appeared to be fading in and out of consciousness. Worry speared through June—he might need a hospital. But it was too late even to consider trying to make it all the way back into town with him in this condition. And then there'd be questions.

The cave house was closer, safer.

"Hey, you," she whispered, lightly slapping the side of his rugged cheek with her palm. "Can you hear me?"

He moaned. His complexion was deathly pale and blood was seeping into the white bandage on his head. The sutures must be pulling loose.

"Listen to me—I'm going call you Jesse, okay? *Jesse,* can you hear me?"

His eyes flickered, as if with sudden recognition.

"Good. Now, stay with me, Jesse. We're almost there."

June's muscles burned as she maneuvered Jesse through the narrow rock crevasse. At the end of the crevasse there was an apparent dead end hidden by a tangle of creepers. June moved the curtain of vegetation aside, exposing the opening to a large cave. These mountains were riddled with them. She clicked on her headlamp, and helping Jesse bend over, they entered the gloom.

"Where are we?" he said.

"A cave. At the back is a tunnel that leads to a valley on the other side. We're going to a shelter built into more caves on that side."

The tunnel was wide, but the roof was low, which meant Jesse leaned even more heavily on June as he was forced to bend double. June's energy began to sag under the weight of well over six feet of Marlboro Man. In close proximity, his stubble rubbed against her cheeks, and June realized peripherally that she had not had a man like this in her arms since Matt had died.

Her pilot had been all rugged brawn and macho power, as well, an A-type personality in total command of his life. Until the one rescue mission that had burned him.

There was always the one mission, thought June. Post-traumatic stress disorder was a little-acknowledged aspect of rescue work, and it often went undiagnosed, as it had in Matt's case. She should have seen it.

She should have given Matt the benefit of the doubt—she should have realized he was incapable of leaving the cult on his own and she should never have given him the ultimatum that had sent him over the edge.

June braced her hand against the cold cave wall as she struggled to catch her breath. She thought she'd managed to put the guilt from the past in perspective, but now it was haunting, so very real again, in the shadows of this cave. It was this stranger—he was doing this to her. Something about his physical presence reminded her too much of the only man she'd ever truly loved. And now the ghosts were coming back.

She glanced at Jesse—when his memory returned, if it returned, would he be friend or foe?

He slumped suddenly to the floor of the cave, trying to grab onto the wall as he went down. June dropped to her knees besides him. His breathing was shallow, his skin cold, clammy. Urgency bit into her.

"Jesse, hang in just a little while longer. We're almost there."

She struggled to help him up, and as they shuffled along, the tunnel grew narrower, darker. Her headlamp started to flicker, the battery dying. Shadows leaped and lunged and the air grew dank, musky. A bat fluttered past her face, making a soft wind.

The journey through the crevasse and tunnel combined was less than a mile, but tonight it felt endless. June's breath was ragged and she was perspiring with the effort. Then suddenly she saw faint light ahead. Relief washed through her body.

They were almost through into Hidden Valley, a narrow delta on the other side of this mountain range. It was inaccessible by road—the only way in was via this secret tunnel or by foot over the mountains, or to fly in by chopper. It was where an eccentric architect-turned-survivalist had chosen to build a large house into a deep warren of caves, and it was in this house the architect had lived, quietly and off-grid, until his death. He'd left everything he owned to his sister, who'd helped turn it into a safe haven for escapees from Samuel Grayson's lethal cult.

The front of the cave house had been walled in with locally sourced rock. Large tinted windows looked out over Hidden Valley, and a stone porch, partially shaded by a rock overhang, ran the length of the house. A narrow boardwalk led from the tunnel entrance and hugged the rock face all the way to the porch and front door. A creek cascaded from a fissure in the rock face and ran under the boardwalk before meandering out into the valley.

The rooms deeper inside the caves had no windows but were vented via stone flues to the ground on top, and the chill inside, even during summer, was eased by a great stone hearth in the central living area and by smaller cast-iron wood-burning stoves in the rooms. When the architect had left the house to his sister, she'd had no idea what to do with it and had let it stand empty; the place had faded from the memory of those who had known about it. When she found out that Hannah Mendes, a relative by marriage, needed a safe house to help cult victims escape, she had offered the cave house as a perfect solution because of the hidden-tunnel access to the valley on the other side.

As June and her injured stranger reached the boardwalk, Jesse passed out. She struggled to hold him, but he slid from her grasp and slumped with a dull thud onto the wooden slats of the walkway. Adrenaline thrummed through her as she checked his pulse. It was steady, and he was still breathing. She worried now about intracranial swelling pressuring his brain.

Laying him in a prone position on the boardwalk, she ran to the house and banged on the door.

"I need help! Can someone come out here and help me!"

The door swung open. Molly, an eighteen-year-old whom June had brought to the safe house last week, stood in the doorway, pulling on her sweater, eyes wide circles of consternation. "What's going on! Did they find us!"

God, I hope not.

"I found a man down a ravine while I was searching for Lacy. He's got a Devotee tattoo, and he's hurt—"

"Is he a henchman?" Molly peered nervously down the boardwalk. "Why did you bring him here! Does he know what happened to Lacy?"

"I don't know who he is. He doesn't remember anything—"

"You shouldn't have brought him here!"

"Molly, calm down and help me carry him. We'll lock him in my room until we stitch him up and learn more."

Molly refused to budge.

"*Molly,* we can't leave him to die out here. Go get Davis and Brad—now!"

The two men came running out into the rain and helped carry Jesse inside.

"Take him to my room!" June yelled as she rushed behind them. "Molly, get me some towels, hot water, the big medical kit from the main bathroom."

June shucked her wet jacket. "Lay him on my bed. Brad, ask your mom to come light the fire in the stove in my room."

She checked Jesse's breathing again—still steady. His pulse was okay, too. June palmed off her wet peaked cap, and Molly pulled a side table alongside the bed atop which she put the medical kit.

June shone a small flashlight into the stranger's eyes. His pupils responded normally, then, as if irritated by the light, he blinked fast, moaning as he came around again.

Relief washed through June. Maybe the guy was just exhausted. She wondered how long he'd actually been in the mountains, how many hours he'd lain, wet and cold, in the ravine, and when he'd last gotten some calories into him. She had to remove his wet clothes, warm him up.

"Molly, please go heat up some of that soup Sonya made the other day—I'm beginning to think our stranger has been walking through the wilderness for some time."

"Why do you want to help him—you said he's a Devotee,

and look, he's got a holster. Only henchmen carry sidearms. He's got to be a henchman."

June shot her a glance. "Do you recognize him? Has anyone in this house seen him before?"

"No."

"Then let's give him the benefit of the doubt, okay?"

The one thing she had not given Matt.

"Just because I don't recognize him from Cold Plains doesn't mean he's not a henchman."

"Molly, just get the soup. And on your way to the kitchen, ask Davis to fetch a change of men's clothing from the closet in the big room. There should be sweatpants and a T-shirt in there large enough to fit him."

June made sure there was always extra clothing in the safe house—she never knew who might arrive in an emergency with only the clothes on their back.

Molly trudged to the kitchen, shoulders set in a sullen slouch. The kid was acting out of fear, thought June as she propped Jesse up on several pillows. Molly was terrified Samuel's reach would extend into the safe house and June couldn't blame her.

"I'm going to get you into some dry clothing, Jesse," she said calmly, maneuvering his wet denim jacket off his shoulders. "Then I'll clean those wounds properly and stitch you up."

He cleared his throat. "You're calling me Jesse—why? Is it my name?" His voice was hoarse.

"That's what your belt buckle says—probably a clothing brand. But I had to call you something." June helped him lift his damp T-shirt over his head.

"Great." His lips almost curved, then he sighed heavily, closing his eyes as he leaned back into the pillows.

His torso was sun-browned, as if he made a habit of working outdoors without a shirt. And his large hands were calloused—a man of physical labor, or a rancher perhaps? June didn't peg this guy as the poolside- or beach-tanning type.

A thick scar curved down one side of his waist, as if he'd been gored by something. Another scar snaked up the inside of his arm.

June frowned. A violent life, or a bad accident of some kind?

But apart from the old scars there were no fresh swellings or lacerations that she could ascertain.

His chest hair was dark. June's gaze followed the whorl of hair that ran down his washboard abs and disappeared seductively into his low-slung jeans. She needed to get him out of those wet pants, and the idea suddenly made her think of sex, which was ludicrous. She was a trained paramedic. The human body was part of her job. She never reacted like this.

Nevertheless, this rugged mountain man was doing it for her, and it made her uneasy.

She glanced up at his face. His eyes were closed, and he was breathing deeply, rhythmically, his bare chest rising and falling. He had a fine scar across his chin, too, and crinkles fanned out from his eyes—smile lines and sad lines. Deep brackets framed his mouth…a beautifully shaped, wide mouth. She couldn't help noticing. Or imagining what it might feel like to have those lips brush hers.

She cleared her throat. "I'm going to get you out of your boots and jeans. Is that okay, Jesse?"

No response. Worry washed softly through her again, and inside her heart compassion blossomed.

She shook his shoulder. *"Jesse?"*

He nodded, eyes still closed.

"Are you just exhausted, or do you have pain anywhere else?"

"Tired," he whispered. "Just…really tired."

June removed his boots and wet socks and quickly unbuckled his belt once more. She edged his pants down over his hips and swallowed.

His thighs were large, all muscle, his legs in stunning shape apart from a massive scar across his left knee—looked as if he'd had some kind of surgery there.

She covered him with a soft blanket, pointedly ignoring the dark flare of hair between his thighs and trying not to think about how well-endowed he was. She put his wet boots in front of the cast-iron stove and hung his jeans over the back of a chair to dry. Flames glowed in the little stove window, and June realized she was perspiring, pulse racing.

She ran her hand over her damp hair, feeling edgy, perturbed. She hadn't wanted sex since she'd lost Matt and had thrown herself wholly into cult and rescue work. And she preferred it that way. It helped her stay focused. She needed every ounce of her focus right now because that dark and rugged stranger lying naked on her bed *could* represent everything she'd devoted her life to fighting—he could be a cult enforcer, violent and potentially deadly to everyone she was trying to protect in this safe house.

June returned to his bedside and looked at him. He wore no wedding band, no jewelery, nothing that could clue her in to his identity. Apart from his watch. She removed it and studied it. It was high-tech, complete with altimeter, barometer and compass, the kind of equipment a serious outdoor enthusiast would wear. Her thoughts turned to his GPS and the route he'd save on it. She made a mental note to get it out of her pack and go through it thoroughly later.

"Do you need anything else?"

June spun round, startled by the male voice.

It was Davis. The middle-aged man had entered the room, placed a pile of clean clothes on the chair next to the bed.

June's face felt hot. "Thanks, Davis. I think we should get someone out to stand guard at the canyon entrance for a while—I'm worried Samuel's men might come looking for this guy, if he is actually one of them, and stumble upon our passageway. Can you do it?"

Davis looked at her oddly. "Are you okay, June?"

"I'm fine," she said a little too crisply. Then she rubbed her brow. "I'm just really worried about Lacy and the twins. I should have found them by now. I—"

"You *will* find them, June. If anyone can, it's you and Eager."

Emotion surged into her eyes, and the burden of responsibility she'd undertaken, the amount of trust these people put in her, was suddenly overwhelming.

"Thanks, Davis."

"I'll take the first watch. Brad can replace me."

"Don't forget to take a radio. And one of the shotguns."

He paused at the door. "You really think they'll come?"

She glanced at Jesse. "I hope not."

I hope I haven't made the biggest mistake in my life by bringing him here.

"Make sure Molly has a receiving radio tuned in to the right frequency. Tell her to keep it with her at all times and to pass it on to someone else if she wants to sleep."

Davis closed the door behind him as he left.

June busied herself cleaning and disinfecting the wounds on Jesse's head and leg. She administered local anesthetic, stitched him up and applied dressing. He remained conscious but in a state of exhausted half sleep, which both puzzled and worried her.

She put dry track pants on him and took a moment to study the tattoo on his hip again.

With surprise she realized the *D* was fresh—maybe only seven to ten days old, the skin around the ink still pink and slightly inflamed.

She frowned. This didn't fit the picture for one of Samuel's henchmen. The enforcers Samuel used tended to be solidly entrenched Devotees who'd proved themselves to him and demonstrated they were able and prepared to defend Samuel's empire violently. Or, at least, those were the henchmen she knew of.

June's chest tightened with conflict as she covered the stranger with more blankets. She packed up her first-aid kit, and suddenly a wave of fatigue hit hard. She told herself it was just the adrenaline wearing off. She still had to go out and look for Lacy and the twins—she'd start along the west flank where she and Eager had found Jesse and his gun. There was no way she'd be able to put in even a cursory appearance with Fargo's search party at this late stage of the morning, so she'd spend her time searching solo with her K9.

Molly entered the room carrying a tray with a bowl of steaming vegetable soup. She eyed Jesse with hostility as she set the tray on the table next to the bed.

June shook his shoulder, gently rousing him. "Jesse—Molly brought you some soup. I think you should get some warmth into you."

His thick lashes fluttered and he turned his head from side to side.

He could hear her voice—soft, sexy, feminine—as if it were coming from a faraway place with warm light. He felt her hand on his bare shoulder—her skin soft, cool. So feminine. He struggled to swim up to full consciousness—to her—and his eyes fluttered open. But everything was a hazy blur, bright. Then slowly, the room came into focus. And he saw her, sitting beside his bed.

An angel. With flaming-red hair. Beautiful, fine-boned features. Porcelain-pale skin brushed by freckles, eyes the color of a pale summer sky that reminded him of the sound of bees and lawn mowers and watermelon by the pool. Her mouth was full, wide. Kissable.

He frowned, trying to place her face, his memories of summers past.

And, as he pulled things into focus, he realized her red hair was damp, tendrils drying in soft spirals around her face. The rest was pulled back in a braid, and there were bits of leaves stuck in it.

He remembered now—it had been pouring. She'd had a peaked cap on when she'd found him, and a headlamp, shining down into his face. Where was he?

He tried to get up. But she gently placed her hand on his shoulder, her willowy body belying a resilient strength he could sense in her touch, see in her clear eyes. He sagged back into the pillows, feeling as though he'd been hit by a ten-ton truck. His head throbbed. His leg hurt—his whole body felt stiff.

"Christ, what happened to me?"

"You fell down a ravine, hit your head and gashed your leg. I've sewn you up and the injuries look fine, but you need to take it easy, Jesse. You've lost blood."

Jesse. That's right—she'd named him Jesse because he couldn't the hell remember who he was, where he was going or where he'd come from. Despair sank into him, along with a bite of frustration.

She was watching him intently. So was the young woman with straight mousey-blond hair she'd referred to as Molly. The kid looked hostile.

What did the redheaded angel with the porcelain skin say her name was…*June.* She'd said she worked as a part-time paramedic in a town called Cold Plains. Thank God—he wasn't completely brain-dead. And he could recall hiking with her assistance through a narrowing rock canyon, into a cave and a tunnel. After that his memory was black again.

Cold Plains. Why did the name of that town seem so familiar, yet not? Another name came to him. *Samuel Grayson.* Tension reared up inside Jesse along with a gnawing urgency. He struggled to sit up—he had to go somewhere, but he couldn't recall where, and it had something to do with a man named Samuel Grayson.

June pressed him gently back against the pillows. "Do you recall those three words I gave you earlier, Jesse?"

What words? Oh, wait…he did remember. He cleared his throat "*Radio, belt* and—" he gave a wry smile "—*Jesse.*"

"Your short-term memory is intact. That's a good sign."

"Yep. Great." *Too bad about the rest.*

"Do you remember anything else, like where you were coming from?"

Frustration heated his body. He tried to dig deeper into his memory, but all he got was a thick sense of fuzzy confusion.

"No, I—I think I was… No, I can't recall a damn thing."

"I checked your GPS. It appears you were traveling into Cold Plains over the north mountains. Do you remember how long you've been in the wilderness? Where you were going? Can you tell me why you have a *D* tattooed on your hip?"

"I have a tattoo?" Had June told him that already—or did the familiarity stem from a buried memory?

"He has the *D* because he's one of Samuel's enforcers," Molly spat at him. "He knows *exactly* what you're talking about, June—he's lying that he doesn't remember anything. Don't fall for it."

June said, quietly, without looking at the young woman, "Molly, can you please go to the kitchen and man the radio. Let me know if Davis reports in."

Molly stomped out of the room and banged the door shut behind her.

"She's afraid," said June.

"Of *me?*"

"Of Samuel Grayson and whoever works for him, and if you're one of his, that includes you."

Samuel. Why did that name strike such a strident cord in him? "Did you tell me about him already, in the ravine?"

"Samuel is the leader of a cult in Cold Plains," June said, assessing him carefully as she spoke. Jesse got the sense she was watching for some kind of reaction to her words, something that would show he was lying. Anxiety curled through him.

"He calls his followers Devotees," she said. "And, as Molly pointed out, he personally tattoos a small *D* on the hip of each one of his true followers." She paused. "None of this sounds familiar?"

The trouble was, it did. But he couldn't figure out why.

"No," he said.

Her mouth flattened and something in her eyes changed. "Earlier you were muttering about Samuel and something urgent you had to do."

Jesse's heart began to race. His mouth felt dry. He did recall that now. But he didn't know what it meant. And he didn't like what was happening here. He glanced at the pistol holstered on her hip, then his gaze went to the door. It struck him there were no windows in this room. Claustrophobia crawled around the edges of his mind.

"I don't remember saying those things." He was lying now, and he knew it. He felt in his gut he had to, but didn't understand why.

"You pulled a gun on me," he said.

Her gaze was steady, cool. "You grabbed me."

He frowned. The action hurt his head. His hand went to his forehead.

"Don't touch." She got to her feet, went over to a dresser that had framed photographs on top. She brought him a handheld mirror.

"You can take a look."

He took the mirror from her, his hand brushing against her cool, slender fingers as he did. Jesse saw a wedding band on her left hand, and felt a sharp and sudden stab of remorse, guilt. Shame.

He glanced at his own hand. No wedding band—not even a tan line. But he felt as if something *should* be there. A deep uneasiness bored down into him. Slowly, he looked into the small mirror.

The face that looked back was familiar. His. But he could attach nothing more to it. She'd done a neat job of the stitches along his brow. A memory hit him. A woman, brunette, running through the dark forest. Rain. She had two young children in her arms. She was screaming hysterically.

Bastard! No henchman is going to get my children!

She had hit him with a branch across his brow.

Gunfire. He could recall shooting. There were men—running through the forest. Then he was falling, falling. Pain in his leg.

Then nothing. Swirling mist, blackness.

Sweat broke out over his torso.

Slowly he lowered the mirror.

Those clear, summer-sky eyes were staring intently at him. She was waiting.

But he said nothing. He was afraid he might have done something—he felt bad about it and he didn't understand why.

She sat on the chair next to the bed and leaned forward, her elbows on her knees, her hands clasped in front of her. A quiet urgency buzzed about her.

"If you remember *anything*, Jesse, you need to tell me—it could help the lives of a mother and her small children."

He looked away. Her black Lab was lying in a basket by the stove, watching him, too. The bed he was lying on was queen-size. There was a closet at the far end of the room. The walls of this room were uneven, and he realized suddenly that they were rock.

"Where am I?"

"A safe place. Look, Jesse, before anything else, I need you to try harder. A young mother in her thirties, brunette, went missing with her three-year-old twin girls in these woods two nights ago." She paused, her intensity sharpening. "Her name is Lacy Matthews and she runs the coffee shop on Main Street in Cold Plains. Her twins are in the local day care. Lacy was a Devotee. Like you, she has a *D* tattooed on her hip. But she wanted to get out of the cult. I was supposed to meet her to bring her to this safe house, but she never showed up."

"You help people escape the cult?"

Her eyes narrowed, and he thought he detected a sliver of fear.

"Yes," she said coolly. "This is a halfway house, a place from where escapees can access exit-counseling, and then go on to start new lives somewhere else."

"*You* do deprogramming?"

"I'm trained to offer early-stage exit-counseling."

The words *cult, Devotee, henchman* circled around and around in Jesse's brain, as if they were important to him. But he couldn't slot them into any bigger picture.

The image of the brunette screaming, fleeing from him, sliced across his brain again, sharp, like pieces of broken mirror.

Jesse swallowed, met her gaze. Was he a bad guy—did he work for Samuel Grayson?

"Did you see Lacy and her daughters, Jesse?"

He cursed, suddenly agitated, angry. "I wish you'd stop asking me the same questions—I don't remember a goddamn thing!"

She watched him in silence for several beats, as if weighing his words for truth.

"If you did see them," she said very quietly, an anger now flickering deep in her eyes, "and if you told me where, I might be able save their lives, if they are even still alive."

His heart hammered and his head pounded. She was repeating herself, pressing him as if she didn't believe him. "Maybe if you searched where you said you found my Beretta," he said quietly.

Her mouth flattened. "I never told you what kind of gun I found."

He said nothing.

She lurched to her feet, hostility, determination in her movements.

"Well, that's *exactly* where I'm going to start searching, Jesse. And believe me, if you've hurt them, I'm going to make you pay. I'm going to make damn sure you go down for it."

He didn't doubt her for a second.

She stalked toward the door, her black Lab surging instantly to follow at her heels, his claws clicking on the polished stone floor. She opened the door. Outside was a passageway, warm light. One hand on the door handle, she turned to face him.

"Someone will be armed with a shotgun and standing right outside. Try anything stupid and they'll shoot you right through the door."

"I'm a prisoner?"

"You're tattooed with the *D* of a Devotee and you were carrying concealed, which implies you could be a cult enforcer. I don't know if you're playing me, or whether you actually have lost your memory, and I don't know what you were doing in the woods where an innocent mother and her children went missing. Until I do know, you're staying where you can't hurt anyone."

"You have no right to keep me locked in this…cave room, or whatever it is."

"Until I can get the FBI, yeah, I figure I've got that right."

June stepped out of the room. She shut the door with a snick. And Jesse heard a key turn in the lock.

Outside the door June leaned back against the cool rock wall and closed her eyes for a moment, trying to gather herself. She'd been rattled by her sharp and instant physical reaction to this rugged stranger she'd found in the woods—a man who could easily turn out to be an archenemy, someone who symbolized everything she detested, everything she'd devoted her life toward fighting.

"Everything okay?"

June blushed and cursed her redhead's complexion. "I didn't hear you coming, Molly. Listen, don't go back into that room, not until I return. He's got what he needs in there and he can use the en suite. Just make sure someone is outside here 24/7 with a loaded shotgun. If he causes trouble, threaten to shoot him through the door."

Molly's lips curved slightly. "I knew you'd see him for what he was. You shouldn't have brought him here, June."

"I couldn't let him die. That's not who I am."

"Then what are you going to do with him?"

"Hand him over to FBI Agent Hawk Bledsoe, but my priority right now is Lacy and the twins. I'll call Hawk when I'm closer to town and within cell-tower range."

"Has Agent Bledsoe actually been to the cave house?"

"He knows it exists, but I haven't brought him or any of the other agents in yet. It hasn't been easy knowing who to trust, Molly—the fewer people who know where the house is the better."

"But you do trust Agent Bledsoe?"

"He's one of the only people out there I can trust. His

sister-in-law is the reason I came to Cold Plains. I don't know about the other agents, though. I haven't wanted to take the risk."

June left Molly standing outside the door as she went to get some dry clothes from the supply closet. She changed into jeans that were too large and cursed herself for not having the foresight to gather clothes from her own room before locking Jesse in—but she wasn't going back in there now.

She checked her gear, fed Eager, grabbed an apple and headed back out into the rain with her dog. But as they reached the entrance to the tunnel, her pager beeped again.

It was Fargo. He was still looking for her. Tension strapped across June's chest. It was just a matter of time before he went looking for her at the ranch, and when he saw her truck there, but no sign of her or her dog, he was going to get suspicious.

The clock was ticking on her cover.

June clicked on her headlamp and ducked into the black tunnel, hoping that rescuing a perfect stranger wasn't going to be her downfall.

Or death.

Chapter 3

Jesse paced in his prison.

He appeared to be in some sort of cave room.

He felt the walls with the palm of his hand—they were definitely natural rock, cold, uneven. But the wall with the door had been constructed of concrete and was smooth and whitewashed, as if perhaps a dwelling had been constructed inside a giant cave and various rooms walled off. The air felt chilled in spite of the fact a fire burned in a black cast-iron stove in the corner. His gaze followed the stove flue up to the roof. It had been vented through a hole hewn into the rock ceiling. There were two more vents in the ceiling at different intervals—possibly to circulate air from the outside.

A small bathroom adjoined the bedroom. Jesse entered. It contained the bare basics—towels, a toothbrush, toothpaste, shampoo, body lotion, a comb and brush with some long red hairs.

No windows anywhere.

Claustrophobia tightened around him. He didn't like the feeling of being underground and his was a prison not only of physical space, but of his own mind. He—the real Jesse, whoever he was—had been locked down somewhere deep inside his brain.

He exited the bathroom and paced the length of the room, then back again, working stiffness from his legs. The wound on his calf hurt, but better to keep it mobile, he thought, or that would stiffen up, too. And as he paced he had to ward off the stifling waves of anxiety induced by being confined in a small space.

Jesse needed wide-open spaces, wilderness, jagged snow-capped peaks…*horses.*

He froze.

Horses, snowcapped mountains—they felt like a part of him. Closing his eyes, he strained to unearth more around the images. But nothing more would come. He tried visualizing himself on a horse. He could almost feel the movement of the saddle, hear the creak of worn leather, the chink of a bridle. He saw a sandy trail unfolding in front of him. He could scent pine and he sensed at his side—within easy reach—a 270 *Winchester.*

Sweat prickled over his body.

That was a very specific piece of information on the rifle, just as he'd known his official sidearm was a newly issued .40 Beretta. He stilled, heart kicking.

Issued.

Official.

He tried to dig even deeper but the clues scurried away from his consciousness into the shadowed crevices of his brain. It frustrated the hell out of him.

The words *cult, Devotee, Samuel, henchman* began to circle through his mind again, and again, and they came with a crushing, devastating sense of loss, guilt. Abandonment. Deception.

Sharp images sliced like shards through his head…the woman running, children screaming. Him raising his gun, anger pumping through his blood. Remorse. Something terrible…*his fault*.

Jesse braced his hands on the dresser, head down, brain spinning, and he closed his eyes, trying to force the memories into his head.

But nothing more would come to him

He slammed his fist onto the dresser.

The photos atop the dresser jumped and one of the frames toppled over. Startled at the force of his own simmering aggression, he picked up the frame to set it back on its stand and realized it was a photo of June. In it, she was crouching next to a man in a flight suit. A child stood between them with his little arms around the neck of a yellow Labrador. The photo had been shot in front of a small helicopter behind which there was dense forest and mountains. *Pacific Northwest, maybe,* thought Jesse.

The man in the photograph with June was tall, athletic build, sandy-blond hair in a buzz cut. His features were angular, his gray eyes sharp. He had his arm around June's shoulders—possessive, protective, yet somehow intimate and loving. Jesse examined the photo more closely. The boy, maybe three years old, looked like the man's son—same eye shape, same color. But the boy's hair was more strawberry blond than sandy.

Jesse's attention shifted to June and her red hair.

She was smiling, her eyes bright, her cheeks pink. Jesse imagined the air must have been cold that day.

She really was beautiful, in a way that he liked—tall, slender, yet possessing a strength and confidence that showed in her athletic body, in her intense gaze, in the way she held her head. Not cutesy-pretty, but sexy as all hell to him. Her hair in this photo was loose and hung in thick, soft waves around her shoulders. He liked redheads.

Jesse swore. How did he know what he liked in a woman?

How could he remember some things about himself without having a full sense of his own identity or where he came from or where he was going? He plunked the photo down and swiveled around, suddenly desperate to get out of here.

He strode over to the door, rattled the handle.

A young female voice sounded from the other side. "Touch that freaking door again and I'll shoot a hole right through it and you!"

It sounded like that kid Molly. She'd probably do it, too.

He spun around and stared at the bed with its functional bedding, the plain rug on the floor, the dog basket near the fire. Given the photo on the dresser, the red hairs in the bathroom, he figured this must be June's bedroom, yet it didn't feel lived-in. Maybe she was just minimalist.

He strode over to the wardrobe standing against the far wall and yanked open the doors. There was a full-length mirror inside. Jesse stared at himself—his bare chest, the scars on his torso and arm. He leaned closer and examined the thin scar across his chin, then he rubbed his jaw. He needed a shave. A good haircut, too.

He angled his body and lowered the gray sweatpants down his hip to examine the small *D* tattoo in the mirror. The skin around it was still pink.

June's soft, sexy voice curled through his mind: *You're a Devotee, Jesse, carrying concealed, a member of the Cold Plains cult…henchman…did you shoot at them, hurt the mother and her children?*

A wave of sickening guilt washed over him.

He glanced up into his own eyes.

Are you hiding from yourself, Jesse? Running from some-thing you don't want to remember?

He flicked the wardrobe door shut and slumped onto the bed, dropping his face into his hands, feeling dizzy, strange.

Did he even want his memory to return?

Was he bad? Had he hurt those twins and their mother?

Was it his fault they were missing?

He honestly didn't know.

Using her GPS, June had tracked back to where she and Eager had found the .40 Beretta.

She now stood in the spot. The light in this dense part of the forest remained dim and mist still fingered through the trees, but the rain had finally abated. It wouldn't be long, though, before the next—and bigger—storm front rolled in. She needed to find Lacy before it did.

June had brought a sealed plastic bag with her. In it was the red shoe and some other belongings she'd taken earlier from Lacy's home. She removed the bag from her backpack now and began to open it. Eager watched attentively. But June stilled when she heard the noise of a twig breaking and then a rustle in leaves. Eager's ears went alert.

June's pulse quickened. She could hear water plopping onto leaves and trickling through cracks in rock. A wind soughed through the treetops, and the trunks of two trees creaked and groaned as bark rubbed together. A squirrel chirped a high-pitched warning at something.

It could have been wildlife breaking the twig, thought June. Or it could be henchmen come to look for their miss-ing comrade. Anxiety torqued through her. She had to work faster.

She held the bag open and let Eager sniff the articles inside.

"This, Eager, find *this*," she said softly.

He nuzzled the articles then started snuffling the ground, living up to his name, eager to find, eager to please. He alerted on something almost instantly, his body wiggling as he pawed at moss.

June crouched down, saw spent shell casings. Her chest tightened. These were 9 mm, not from the .40 Beretta—which meant they hadn't been fired from Jesse's gun, *if* it was truly his. She was beginning to doubt everything now.

She photographed and bagged the casings, this time in paper bags she'd brought from the safe house. If there were fingerprints or DNA on these casings, plastic would compromise the evidence. She put the bags in her pack and began to work Eager up the mountain, through the trees, toward the base of the cliff from where the wind was coming. Eager indicated again, this time on a log about the thickness of an arm.

Around the log June found broken leaves, scuffed loam, crushed ferns. Using a stick, she rolled the log over. On its underside was something dark, sticky, looked like blood. Beside it, another shell casing glinted in the loam—a .40 caliber. This one could have come from the Beretta. And there was more blood on the underside of the leaves.

Had Jesse shot and injured Lacy here? She didn't even want to contemplate the little twins being hurt. She inhaled deeply, trying to temper her adrenaline.

"Good boy, Eager," she whispered, ruffling the fur on his chest. She took hold of his collar and she said, "Do you want to find more? Are you *ready?* Are you ready, boy? *Search!*"

She let him go and he was off like a rocket again. June ran after him, feeling the weight of her backpack, her hiking boots like lead on her feet—she was more tired than she'd realized. Her pager went off again. She stopped, catching her breath as she quickly checked it.

Bo Fargo, yet again.

Had he been to the ranch yet? Seen her truck? Questioned Hannah? But before she could think further, June saw something change in Eager's posture—a slight pop of his head in a new direction, fresh tension in his body, his tail wagging loosely. He was onto human scent, and he was making a beeline for a tangle of thick vegetation along the base of the cliff wall.

He started barking excitedly.

June caught up to him and grabbed his collar. "Lacy?" she whispered into the bushes.

A harsh whisper sounded from inside the brush. "*June?* Is that you!"

Eager started to bark louder.

"Good boy, Eager! Where's Lacy? Show me!"

Panting with excitement, he wiggled his muscular body through the tight brush. June followed. Twigs pulled at her hair, dislodging her peaked hood as she pushed through.

And there they were, Lacy and the twins, huddled together in a small cave hidden by the scrub.

"June! Oh, thank God, it is you!" Lacy threw her arms around June and began to sob with relief as Eager wiggled about them, tail thumping in pride. The twins—Abby and Bekka—sat dead-silent, watching wide-eyed.

"Thank you for coming," Lacy whispered, finally pulling herself away, wiping her eyes with shaking hands. Her face was as pale as a ghost's, her eyes dark holes, her hair and clothes bedraggled. Her little bundle of gear rested next to her children.

June moved quickly toward the kids.

"Are you guys okay?" she said, noting that at least their shelter was dry, and they'd had some food, judging by the granola wrappers and a juice bottle on the dirt next to them. June took the Dorothy slipper out of her pack.

"Look what I brought, girls. One of your Dorothy shoes.

And I know where the other one is, too." June smiled shakily, her own eyes pricking with moisture as she offered the shoe to Abby. "I can get the other one for you, then we can click the heels together and you'll all be in a safe and warm place, okay?"

The child stared with huge brown eyes. Then suddenly she lunged forward, her little arms wrapping as tightly as a limpet around June's neck.

Tears flowed down June's cheeks, emotion racking through her body. She hugged the child as tightly as she dared, closing her eyes, thanking the universe that this time, she hadn't lost a child, but saved two.

It made losing her own little Aiden just a bit more bearable. It gave his short life just a little more value—because of him, because of what had happened to Matt, June was here right now, in this cave, helping this mother and her children. And she knew what she was doing was right.

June pulled back, wiping her face with the back of her hand. She needed to stay strong. She needed to get this little family all the way back through the dark tunnel and into the safe house. Before anyone else arrived.

"What happened, Lacy? Why didn't you show up at the meeting place? Are you *sure* you're all okay?"

"We're just cold, tired, scared. We had some granola bars and juice." She stared to cry again. "I always carry juice and stuff for the twins."

Placing her hand on Lacy's shoulder, June said, "That's what mothers do. It's okay, Lacy. I'm going to get you all somewhere safe, but you need to tell me everything that happened so I know what we're dealing with."

"I—I tried to go to the big black rock sentinel where Hannah said you'd come meet us. We were a bit early, and as we were coming up the trail, we heard voices. I ducked down, told the twins to stay put, and I crept forward. I saw two henchmen through the branches, patrolling the area. They had rifles and handguns."

"They were waiting at the rock sentinel?"

Lacy nodded.

Anxiety punched through June. "How did they know about the rock?"

"I don't know!"

"It's okay, Lacy. I'm not blaming you…I just need to know."

It could mean we have a mole, or that Hannah's security has been compromised.

"And you're sure they were henchmen?" said June

"*Yes!* I've seen them before, going into Samuel's underground room at the community center. They both used to work for Charlie Rhodes, before he was shot. The one's name is Jason Barnes—he's good friends with a girl named Monica Pearl—and the other guy they call Lumpy because of how beaten up he's gotten in the past."

June thought of Jesse and his scars.

"And what happened when you saw them?"

Lacy moistened her lips. "We started to sneak away, deeper into the forest. After a while I didn't know where we were. Then it got dark. We hid in the forest for the night, and in the morning we started moving again, but I realized we'd gotten turned around somehow and were lost. That's when the rain started. I wasn't sure what to do. I thought maybe the whole safe house and everything had been compromised, and I knew we'd be in trouble if I tried to find our way back to the village." Tears ran afresh down her cheeks. "I was so scared for my babies."

June comforted her. The twins were holding on to Eager. He was doing his job as a good Labrador: Loving people. Licking their faces. Lacy reached out to touch him, and June noticed that her usually perfectly manicured nails were chipped and broken. Her hair, always so impeccably styled, was in disarray. She looked so vulnerable, and in that moment June hated Samuel and his followers with such raw passion it frightened her.

"Then last night," Lacy was saying, "while we were looking for somewhere dry and warm to hide, they must've heard us, and they started running toward us in the dark. I picked up the twins—that's when we dropped the other shoe—and I tried to run, carrying them. But I fell, and by the time I got up, one of them, another man, was coming from the opposite direction." Her jaw tightened and her eyes glittered. "He… he tried to tell me to stop, asked me where I thought I was going in the dark." She sucked in a huge breath.

"I didn't even give him a chance. I wasn't going to let them take my babies. I picked up a huge log and, I swear, superhuman strength filled my body as I swung that sucker right at his face. I screamed at him that no henchman of Samuel's was going to hurt me or my children. He went down like a rock, but then I heard the other two coming up behind him. The henchman on the ground went for his sidearm, but I just picked up my twins and ran for our lives. I could hear him shooting at us as we went."

"So there were *three* men?"

She nodded.

"And no one came after you once you'd hit one of them with a log?"

"No. I—I guess maybe they stopped to help the hurt guy."

"What did he look like, the guy you hit?"

"I—" She exhaled heavily. "I don't really know. I was in a panic. It was dark. But he was big, tall. Denim jacket."

"Dark or fair, can you remember?"

"Dark hair, definitely dark."

June bit her lip. "Would you recognize him, do you think, if you saw him again?"

"I don't know. Maybe. But I hope I never see him again. I hope he's dead."

"Lacy, we need to move quickly, before Samuel's men come back." June picked Bekka up as she spoke. The child was petite, light as a feather, and June's heart ached as memories of her own child swelled inside her. She sucked air in deeply. She had to keep sharp focus if she was to get these two precious little bundles and their mother out of trouble and into the safe house.

Lacy gathered up Abby.

"Let's click heels to go someplace safe, shall we?" said June to the twins.

Abby smiled and nodded, and Bekka chuckled. It warmed June's heart and it steeled her resolve.

With Bekka on June's hip and Lacy carrying Abby, they edged cautiously out the cave and through the undergrowth. Eager panted happily, taking up the rear. June checked her GPS bearings, and figured they could hug a route along the cliff base and cut back across the forest to where they could access the tunnel.

They reached the cave house by noon. An hour later, the twins had been fed, bathed and were sound asleep in the room that functioned as a nursery. There was a bed in the nursery that Lacy would use, too. But she was still wound up on adrenaline and was now sitting with June and Sonya and Tiffany at the big wooden table in the kitchen, a large mug of herbal tea cradled in her hands.

Molly was back on her guard shift outside Jesse's door, and Davis was doing another round of sentinel duty at the canyon entrance. Brad was sleeping so he could take up a night shift if necessary. A two-way radio rested on the table within June's reach.

Lacy knew Sonya—a soft and rounded woman in her

forties who'd "disappeared" from the Cold Plains hardware store—fairly well. She also knew Tiffany, Brad's mother. Tiffy was a secretary at the school. Molly and Davis she'd seen around town. Cold Plains was a small and intimate community, and every good Devotee attended Samuel's seminars.

"I can't believe you got them all out, that they're all *here*," Lacy said in wonderment, her gaze scanning the room.

Above the kitchen table hung a huge chandelier made of antlers. Other lamps had hide shades. June was a vegetarian. She'd have preferred the decor to be, as well, but it was the least of her concerns right now.

"How do you get electricity in here?" said Lacy, looking up at the chandelier.

"Solar panels, up on the cliff," answered June

"This place is so awesome—it's kind of artsy, yet rugged. I really love it."

"Lacy, I need you to—"

But suddenly Lacy began to cry. "I just don't know what's going to happen to my coffee shop now, the staff…it had all seemed so perfect, the town, the people. I so *badly* wanted to believe in it all. I feel so cheated, so deceived. So damn angry that I let myself get sucked up like that."

"Lacy." June placed her hand on the young woman's arm. "Your reaction is normal. I'm going to start you on some exit-counseling and then we'll get you into a program where you can talk to people who understand exactly what you're going through right now. They'll help you work through everything you're feeling, and you're going to be fine. Abby and Bekka are going to be fine. The FBI is finally going to get something to nail Samuel. They *know* he's bad, they *know* what he's doing—it's just a matter of finding evidence they can use in court to effectively prosecute him. He's smart, but the noose is tightening. In the meantime, I need you to do something for me. I need you to be strong, okay?"

Lacy glanced up, wiped her eyes. And June could see the resolve in her face. This young woman, a social butterfly who loved material things, had chucked it all to save her kids and herself. She'd made a bold move, braver than many in town were capable of. June's heart went out to her, and it bolstered her own resolve.

"What you've done, Lacy, gives me faith in what we're trying to do. It makes me believe we're going to see Samuel and his sick empire taken down."

Lacy bit her lip and nodded.

June leaned forward. "But there is just one more thing I need you to do, Lacy. Eager and I found an injured man in the forest last night. He'd fallen down a ravine and had a bad gash across his forehead. He can't recall what happened and he doesn't know who he is."

Lacy's face went sheet-white. *"Henchman?"*

"I can't be sure. He does have a tattoo—"

"And you brought him in here! Where my twins are!"

"Lacy, easy. There are some things about him that don't add up. I need you to see if you recognize him."

Her eyes, unwavering, huge, glared at June.

"Will you come take a look at him, Lacy?"

"I can't!" Her hands pressed flat on the table. "I just can't."

"You can, Lacy. He's hurt, he's lost his memory and he's unarmed. You're safe here. I'll have my weapon with me. Molly will be right outside the door with the shotgun. And I swear, Eager will take him down if he so much as even tries to lift a finger against us."

Doubt flickered through Lacy's features. "June, please, don't make me do—"

"I'll bring Brad and Tiffany and Sonya in with us. I want you all to take a real hard look at this guy and tell me if you might have seen him in Cold Plains before. There'll be safety in our numbers."

June wanted to watch Jesse's face, too, when she brought Lacy and the others in to see him. She'd be looking for a flicker of recognition in his eyes, anything that might indicate he was lying about his memory loss.

The group waited outside June's locked bedroom. Lacy fidgeted nervously. June took a deep breath and rapped on the door.

"Jesse—I'm going to come in," she yelled. "Can you go sit on the bed, please, and stay there while we enter? I have some people I want you to meet."

Silence.

"Jesse?"

"Yeah, yeah, I hear you," he yelled back, and June could hear the irritation in his voice. "I'm on the bed, sitting nice and still. You can come in now."

"I am armed," she warned, nerves skittering through her stomach suddenly. "And so is the guard who will remain right outside your door. Try anything and you're dead, understand? Because I *will* kill you rather than let you hurt these people here."

"I said I hear you," he growled from inside.

She drew her Glock and unlocked the door. Gun leading, Eager in a tight heel at her left side, June stepped inside.

But she stalled at the sight of him sitting on her bed.

He'd put on the white T-shirt Davis had left for him, and it was stretched taut across his honed pecs. His hair had dried into a roguish tumble and his indigo-blue eyes crackled with anger. His whole body seemed to vibrate with a quiet electricity.

June swallowed and met his gaze as she motioned for Lacy to step inside.

His eyes narrowed slightly at the sight of Lacy, but his features betrayed nothing else.

"It's him!" hissed Lacy, grabbing June's arm. "He's the one who tried to stop me. He shot at us."

"Are you sure?"

"Damn right, I'm sure. You bastard!"

"You can leave now, Lacy. Tell the others to come in."

Brad and Tiffany entered the room, followed by Sonya. Both Molly and Davis had already told June they didn't recognize Jesse.

"Have you seen him before?" June asked, her attention fixed on Jesse's face.

There were murmurs of denial.

"Thanks, guys, you can go. Tell Molly to stay outside with the gun."

"Are you sure, June?" Brad whispered, casting a leery glance at Jesse, who sat totally motionless, muscles taut.

"I'm sure."

Once she was alone with him, she said, "That was Lacy. I found her and the twins—"

"Congratulations." His voice was bitter.

"She told me that you tried to block her escape. She hit you across the face with a log, then you shot at her while she fled. I found a log with blood on it, and spent casings, .40 caliber, likely from your Beretta."

He glowered at her.

She felt hot.

"Why did you try to kill Lacy and her children, Jesse?"

"I didn't."

"How can you say that with such unequivocal assertion, yet you can't recall anything about what happened preceding the blow to your head?"

He lurched up, neck wire-tense. "Because I know, dammit! I just *know*…I don't kill people!" He pointed at the door. "Especially not a woman and her children." His hand went suddenly to his brow.

"*What,* Jesse, *what* are you remembering?"

He inhaled deeply. "Look, maybe I have some recall of a brunette and her kids running through the dark, but I feel no urge inside me, no whisper, not one damn thing that tells me I wanted to, or needed to, or did anything to hurt that woman. Nothing. Just…just…" He turned away.

"Just what?" June said.

"I can't place it." There was dejection in his voice now. "But I feel guilt. I feel responsible for something awful that involves a woman, maybe not her, maybe some other woman."

He turned back and his eyes met June's. The raw honesty in them took her aback and her heart clenched. She'd seen a similar look of need, anguish, desperation, in Matt's eyes when she'd told him to choose between her or his religious cult. It was the night before he'd kidnapped Aiden from day care and fled with him into the wilderness.

June had never seen either alive again.

If she'd understood the desperation in Matt's eyes, if she'd been kinder, if she'd sought proper therapy for him, he and Aiden might still be alive. She tried to swallow the sudden sharp surge of emotion swelling inside her, but couldn't.

"There you have it," Jesse said. "I'm opening up, being as honest as I can. What in hell else can I do?" He sank back down onto the bed.

Empathy swelled through June. She sheathed her Glock, and tentatively sat on the edge of the bed beside him.

"Jesse?" she said gently.

He didn't look at her.

She reached out, placed her hand over his.

He stared at her hand, her pale skin against his dark tan, then he looked slowly into her eyes, and she imagined the warmth of his lips against hers. June's stomach swooped and heat pooled low in her belly.

Her raw, physical response to him shocked her. What on earth was going on with her?

A wry smile twisted his lips. "You know what? When I woke up in your bed I thought I was drowning, but then I saw your face and I thought I was seeing an angel. You were surrounded by warmth, light. It made we want to come back up."

Her cheeks went hot. She wanted to remove her hand from over his, but couldn't.

He glanced around the room. "Now I'm in some prison."

"Just until we know who you—"

"I'm not talking about these walls, I'm imprisoned in my own head. What if I never find out who I am? What if this has more to do with a psychological block than an injury to my brain? What if I'm running from something inside myself?"

Silence filled the space between them, loaded, simmering. His skin was hot under her fingertips. He leaned closer, too close. "What does that tell you about me, June?" he whispered.

She got up quickly, heart racing. "I'm just a paramedic, not a doctor. Or a psychologist."

He stared at her for several beats, and June knew he'd seen the unbidden flare of lust in her eyes. She felt naked. Afraid, suddenly, at what was happening inside her.

"I need to talk to Lacy again," she said, making for the door.

"You can't hold me here."

June paused, hand on the doorknob. "I won't, not for long. I'm going to bring in the FBI."

"I don't want to see the feds."

"If you're innocent you won't have anything to worry about, right?"

"I told you, June, I don't know why I feel guilt. Maybe I have done something bad. Maybe I've broken the law in some small way. But I'd like to know who I am, and what I did, before you turn me in."

"You need to see a proper doctor, Jesse. The FBI can help with your ID and with getting you medical care."

"June, help me figure it out before turning me over to the feds."

She scrubbed her hand over her brow. He could be a con artist, playing her. Her gaze flickered to the photo on mantel. Jesse followed her eyes.

"Where is he—your husband?" he said.

She tightened her mouth. She shouldn't answer. That's how they did it—con artists. Little by little, they found your weak points, zeroed in. Then they had you. It's how Samuel had done it with every one of his Devotees.

"He died," she said quietly. "Five years ago."

"You still wear a wedding band."

"To remember why I do what I do."

"What exactly is it that you do, June?"

Without answering, she stepped out the door, locking it behind her.

And June realized her hands were shaking.

Jesse stared at the closed door, heart banging hard against his ribs.

She was a widow—why did it mean so much to him?

His thumb worried his own naked ring finger and desperation swelled in his chest, followed by an indescribable sense of loss and loneliness.

He needed to find the reasons for his feelings of guilt and remorse, and he had to do it before June brought in law enforcement. And he sure wasn't going to find them holed up in here. If he was going to find answers anyplace, it would be in Cold Plains. Jesse needed to go there, and he had to find Samuel. Everything was tied to Samuel.

He lurched to his feet, banged on door. "June!"

No response.

He banged again, then jiggled the lock.

"I'll shoot your ass off!" came Molly's voice.

Jesse didn't doubt it.

He was trapped. At June's mercy. In some cave room. Inside his head.

Chapter 4

June heard him banging as she went down the passage and her jaw tightened, hands fisting at her sides. She wasn't going to be able to contain him in there much longer. She could even face legal implications down the road. Her pager sounded again.

Tension strapped tighter across her chest.

Now that she'd found Lacy, she needed to head down the mountain, back to Cold Plains, to her job. What in hell excuse was she going to give Bo Fargo?

She couldn't tell him she was out of pager range. Although there were dead cell-phone zones in these mountains, the pager system had greater reach.

She entered the living room, which opened out onto the kitchen. Gray light streamed down from skylights and a fire crackled in the stone hearth to ward off the underground coolness that permeated the cave house. It was safe to burn wood now, with the cloud socked low over the mountains—

no telltale smoke would be seen from afar. Otherwise, they burned only at night.

June found Lacy pacing in front of the fire, rubbing her arms in a nervous gesture.

"I need sleep, June—but I can't rest with that man in the same house as my twins. I just can't." Accusation, bitterness filled her eyes. "I don't know why you brought him here. Maybe I should have stayed in Cold Plains. At least if I'd stuck it out with Samuel my children would be safe."

June took hold of Lacy's shoulders. "Look at me, Lacy. That's exactly where Samuel gets his power—by subtly threatening violence or death for disobeying him. He's a sociopath. He's sick—evil. And his is the worst kind of mental abuse. It's no way to live, and you know it. You did the right thing, for your children, for yourself, for your future. I'm going to get you into an exit-counseling program real quick, okay? Which will mean moving you out of the house as soon as we can."

"I thought you did the counseling yourself."

"I do some of the initial work, yes, but I want you to get out of here and into a good program as soon as is feasible."

She sniffed, wiping her nose. "Why? Because I'm more vulnerable than the others?"

"No, Lacy, it's because you've been through an incredibly stressful experience in those woods, and you have your children to think of. You *all* need critical-incident stress counseling as much as you need deprogramming work. Your fear right now is your worst enemy."

Tears filled Lacy's eyes and June hesitated over what she was going to say next, but decided she had to press forward. "Lacy, I need you to walk me through what happened in the woods just one more time. Can you do that?"

Lacy's mouth thinned.

"Please," June said. "Come sit here by the fire. I know you're tired, but this is important."

Lacy lowered herself into a chair next to the hearth, her hands clutching the armrests. June drew up an ottoman, sat in front of Lacy and took her hands. They were ice-cold. Her face was ghost-white.

"Close your eyes," June said gently. "Try to go back to when you first saw the two men near the rock sentinel. What did the air feel like on your face?"

Lacy was silent for a few minutes, then she inhaled deeply.

"It felt damp, full of moisture."

"What could you smell?"

"Soil. Pine needles…" She hesitated, then smiled. "And cherry. Bekka was eating a candy. She smelled like sugar and artificial cherry flavor."

"This is good, Lacy, really good." June was careful to keep her voice calm, soothing. "Now you see the two men—tell me what you're seeing."

"I'm looking at them through bushes—berry bushes, I think. The boughs from the conifers are hanging low. I'm peering through them."

"What's the ground underfoot like?"

"Squishy. Quiet. No noise giving us away."

"Are you holding the twins now?"

She shook her head. "I told them to wait a few yards back. They were so quiet in the forest, the two of them. They must've read my fear." A tear slipped out from under her lashes. "I guess that's where Abby dropped the first shoe."

"And that's where I found it, Lacy. I took it and planted it on the east flank of the hill so they'd think you went in that direction. That's where Bo Fargo, his men and the other SAR volunteers are searching right now. They don't know you're here. You're safe."

Another tear slipped out from under Lacy's lashes and

tracked slowly down her pale cheek. "I saw Jason Barnes and that guy Lumpy."

"Monica Pearl's friend?"

She nodded. "They were standing near the tall black rock sentinel where Hannah told us to wait for you. From there you were supposedly going to lead us to the safe house. But we were early."

June swallowed. "And Jason and Lumpy had guns?"

"Rifles and pistols in their holsters. They were pacing in front of the rock, as if waiting for someone—me—to arrive."

"And you never told a soul you were coming here?"

"Not even Gemma Johnson, and she's the one who helped me see the Devotees for what they really are."

A sinister sense unfurled in June. She had to check on Hannah, see that nothing had happened, or that her cover hadn't been blown. Glancing at the clock on the mantel above the fireplace, she said to Lacy, "And that's when you backed away, sneaked off into the woods."

"Yes."

A banging resounded from down the corridor—Jesse trying to get out. Molly could be heard yelling back at him. Tension wound tighter.

"Let's go right to where you encountered the man in the denim jacket. What was the scent in the forest like there?" June said, trying to get her to go deeper in a form of cognitive interview.

"Still wet, loamy. It was raining heavily, and it was dark, misty. He...the man, just appeared, looming out of the forest, blocking my way. I—I guess his backpack made him seem even bigger than he was."

June's heart kicked. "Backpack?"

"A large one. Like one of those backcountry camping things you take when you go out for a couple of days, with a tent and sleeping roll."

June frowned. There had been no backpack near Jesse. Eager would have found it. Could Jason and Lumpy have taken it? Did it have identification in it?

Blowing out a deep breath, June asked calmly, "What was the first thing Jesse said to you when he appeared in the dark?"

"He...held up the palms of his hands, like this," Lacy said, lifting her hands. "And he said, 'Whoa, where are you off to in such a hurry?' Then he looked at my twins, and he—" Lacy paused, surprised. "He appeared startled, concerned."

"As if he didn't expect to see you and your kids in the dark, rainy woods?"

"God, maybe." She opened her eyes and put her hands to her face. "I...didn't notice that at the time. I just dropped Bekka and Abby on the ground, lifted the first thing I could find, a log, and swung it at him."

"And what did he do then, exactly?"

Lacy made a motion, arms defensively going up to her face, ducking back.

"He ducked from you?"

"I guess. I was in panic, not thinking clearly."

"Close your eyes again, Lacy. Tell me what happened next."

She inhaled deeply. "I yelled at him, saying, 'No henchman of Samuel's is going to hurt my babies.'"

"You said all those words?"

Lacy nodded. "He reeled from the blow and then went down like a rock. I heard the others coming from behind him, crashing through the woods. I dropped the log and picked up Bekka and Abby, one on each hip, my bag over my shoulder, and I just ran. He started shooting at me."

"Did any bullets hit near you?"

"I was too busy running to notice. It was dark. I didn't

want to fall. My only instinct was to get away as fast as I could."

June thought of the .40 caliber shell casings she'd found near the log with blood on it, not far from where Jesse appeared to have fallen down into the ravine. The 9 mm casings were a distance away from that spot.

She bent forward. "Lacy, was there *any* chance Jesse could have been shooting at the other two men and not you? *Could* he have been trying to protect you instead of hurt you? And they fired on him because of it?"

Tears ran fast down Lacy's face now. "I—I suppose…"

"Lacy, listen to me, you did a great thing. And thank you for doing this. Now go try and get some sleep."

Lacy's gaze darted nervously to the passage that led to June's room.

"I can't sleep with him in here."

"He might not be a bad guy, Lacy. You just told me that yourself. We have to give him the benefit of the doubt. He might be lost and in trouble, too."

"We don't know for sure."

We sure as hell don't.

"That's why we're going to keep him locked up with a guard outside that door until the FBI takes him away. I'll call Agent Hawk Bledsoe when I go into town."

"You're *leaving?*" Panic showed in her face.

"I need to put in an appearance, cover my bases. It might take some hours, but you'll be safe with everyone else here."

Lacy got up from her chair. "Are you sure?"

"Hundred percent." June forced a smile. "Trust me, everything is going to work out fine."

June watched the young woman walk out of the living room. She wished she believed her own words.

A white polo shirt enhanced Samuel Grayson's tan, which in turn brought out the vivid green of his eyes. His dark hair was impeccably cut—he was movie-star handsome, and he knew it as he stood in front of his office window waiting for Mayor Rufus Kittridge to arrive. He'd positioned himself so the sun coming through the window would backlight him. It gave him an edge and sent a subliminal message of superiority, godliness. He used lighting to similar effect when he gave his seminars.

A bottle of his Cold Plains Creek "tonic" water had been carefully positioned on his desk beside a clean glass. The creek was the reason Samuel had chosen Cold Plains to establish his business five years ago. Legend dating back centuries claimed water from the creek possessed rejuvenating and healing properties. It was this legend that Samuel sold.

His Devotees bottled the creek water for him out of a sense of duty to their community. And he sold the bottles back to them at $25 a pop, usually at his seminars where peer pressure helped them fork over the dollars. Samuel personally pocketed a hundred percent of the profits. He was now shipping a set quota of bottled water to other towns, too. It was a nicely growing concern.

A rap sounded at his oak door.

"Come in!"

Mayor Rufus Kittridge, in his fifties, limped into the room. His face was round, friendly, and the touch of gray at his temples bespoke experience. The limp was all that remained from injuries sustained in a car-bomb attempt on his life three months ago. Jonathan Miller, the demolitions expert responsible for the bomb, had since been taken into custody in Cheyenne.

"Rufus!" Samuel said warmly as he stepped forward and clasped the man's hand.

The mayor had a firm grip and easy smile. Everyone in town knew him to be a keen Devotee, but few knew their congenial mayor also oversaw two groups of Samuel's militia-style enforcers. One of the groups was headed by Lumpy Smithers, who'd taken over from Charlie Rhodes after Charlie was shot during an FBI raid on the community center. The other group was headed by the deceptively sweet Monica Pearl. Compartmentalization was key to keeping the unsavory—but necessary—deeds committed by the groups at a legal arm's length from Samuel. If the FBI ever got evidence on any of the murders, it would be Rufus, Monica and Lumpy who went down—nothing would stick to Samuel. He was incredibly careful about that.

But he *was* worried right now.

Special Agent Hawk Bledsoe and his FBI team were closing in. On top of this, a total of eleven Devotees had disappeared without a trace in the past three months. And these were *not* "disappearances" sanctioned by him.

Samuel had begun to fear that he had a mole—possibly even a network—working on the inside to get vulnerable Devotees out of Cold Plains, and he'd heard rumors of a safe house.

Under Samuel's orders, Rufus had engaged eighteen-year-old Molly Rigg to pose as a Devotee desperate to get out, and it seemed to have worked—Molly had vanished. But she'd made no contact with Rufus or his men, and Samuel was beginning to fear she'd been deprogrammed. The idea enraged him.

And now Lacy Matthews and her kids had gone missing. The whole town was abuzz with talk of her disappearance from the coffee shop, which was a gathering place, and Samuel needed to quell the fire, make an example of Lacy and her twins, fast.

This was why he'd summoned Rufus to his office.

Before she'd vanished, Lacy had written some words on a notepad in the coffee shop and then ripped off the page.

However, the imprint of her words had remained on the pad. They'd read: "Black rock sentinel, west flank @ 7:00 p.m."

Police Chief Bo Fargo's men had found the notepad, and Fargo had reported the find to Samuel.

He cut right to the point. "Are you sure your men were waiting at the right location?"

The smile on Rufus's face faded.

"It's the only big black rock on the west flank that could be called a sentinel. Lacy never arrived. My men found her around 1:00 a.m. She was screaming at a stranger in the woods but fled as my guys approached. The stranger fired on my guys. One of his bullets hit Jason Barnes in the neck. Lumpy Smithers returned fire. He thinks he hit him because he fell down into a ravine."

"*Thinks* he hit him?"

Rufus remained silent.

Samuel smiled benignly. "Did they look for him?"

"Lumpy made the decision to bring Jason into the hospital right away—he was hurt bad."

Samuel inhaled, slowly. "I presume they got a good look at this stranger's face?"

"No, they did not—"

"What do you mean?"

Rufus moistened his lips.

"It was dark, raining," he said. "The situation was fluid. Lumpy returned to the site where the man had gone down the ravine, but there was no one there."

"So the Matthews woman escaped, and so did this unidentified stranger?"

Rufus cleared his throat. "We do have his backpack—he dropped it."

"Any ID in it?"

"No." Rufus eyed the water on Samuel's desk. "The pack contained food, maps, survival blanket, tent, sleeping bag—

he appears to have been on an extended hike through the wilderness. But no ID."

Samuel opened the bottle of water on his desk as he spoke, poured a glass, then sipped without offering any to Rufus. "The priority was to get the woman and her twins, not Jason Barnes," he said calmly.

Rufus met his gaze. "Jason's condition was critical."

"Damn!" Samuel slammed his glass down. "Jason's not likely going to make it out of ICU, anyway. He's going to die, *and* the woman got away! Get back out there, find her!"

"We're looking. One of the kids' shoes was found on the east flank of the mountain," said Rufus. "We have police and SAR crews combing that area."

"The rock sentinel is on the west flank, and you said your men saw her on that west flank at 1:00 a.m. How do you explain the kid's shoe on the east side?"

"Maybe she fled in that direction."

"Get back out onto the west side with a search party of your own. I want that woman, and I want that stranger. Dead or alive. And keep it quiet that you're looking on that side, understand?"

"Yes, sir." Mayor Rufus Kittridge did not look a happy man.

"And what about Molly Rigg? What happened to our damn mole!"

Rufus smoothed his hand over his hair. "We're still waiting for contact."

Samuel abruptly turned his back on Rufus and stared out the window. It was the mayor's cue to leave.

But as Rufus reached the thick oak door, Samuel said suddenly, "Who found the red shoe on the east flank?"

"June Farrow and her K9."

He did not turn around to face the mayor. "Is she there with the search party now?"

"I would assume so."

Rufus Kittridge exited and closed the door quietly behind him.

Samuel stared into the street. Smiling people walked the sidewalk, greeting each other with respectability. They were his people, it was his town, and it was a clean one—nothing like it had been five years ago before he'd run the drunks and cowboys out.

These people had a lot to thank him for, and he was not going to see a group of renegades taking him down. He made a mental note to ask Fargo about June Farrow and the red shoe.

June attended most of his motivational seminars, but she was not yet a full Devotee. It was time she came to a personal consultation. He wanted to get inside Ms. Farrow's pretty red head—she was a dark horse, newish in town. Samuel didn't feel he knew her well enough.

He glanced at his gold designer watch. It was time for his specially scheduled seminar entitled How to Identify the Enemy Within and Stop It from Sabotaging Efforts to Be the Best You.

June raced up the bank to where Bo Fargo and the SAR team had set up command. Fargo was talking to one of the volunteers under a temporary awning where maps, a coffee urn and radios littered a portable table. It was spitting rain again, more big black clouds rolling in over the mountains.

Fargo caught sight of June and turned to face her as she approached.

He was a big and imposing man in his fifties who'd been widowed mysteriously some years ago.

"I've been trying to reach you," he said, his watery blue gaze running over her.

"I'm sorry, Bo," she said, breathless. "Eager was bitten by

something yesterday and I had to take him to the vet over in
the next town."

"Bitten?"

"I don't know what got him. He swelled right up. He
couldn't breathe. I administered antihistamine but he just
got worse—"

"Your truck was still at Hannah's place."

So he'd been to look. This was not good.

"I was too stressed to drive. I got a ride from Hannah."

"What's wrong with the vet in Cold Plains?"

"The local vet and I have had—" She inhaled, her brain
racing. "Look, it's personal, Bo."

"How so?"

June reminded herself Fargo was a Devotee, one of Samuel
Grayson's main men. Everyone was supposed to get along
happy-happy in this smiling facade of a town, and it was
making her so damn tired and angry.

"The vet and I have different perspectives on treatment,"
she said quietly. "But it's not something we can't work out
as we move forward. In fact, I'm going to go around and see
him again later, because it's so much easier keeping all our
business in town." June forced a smile. "I learned that the
hard way last night. The vet in the town over is not all he's
cracked up to be, either."

"Who is he? Which town?"

She glanced at her watch. "Look, Bo, I really need to get
to this special seminar Samuel is putting on." She met his
gaze. "I got a serious shock with Eager and I could do with
some motivational bolstering right now. Since I don't have
my dog with me, can you manage today's search without us,
while I go sit in on the seminar?"

Bo Fargo studied her. She knew she looked like a wreck.

"I've been in a state," she said for emphasis.

"How's the dog now?"

"He's going to be okay. Vet is keeping him overnight to be sure."

His watery eyes narrowed—he wasn't totally buying her story. She was on thin ice here.

"I'm beat, Bo. I just—"

"Go," he said. "Leave things to us."

She took the gap and rushed off, feeling his eyes burning into her back as she went. He was going to put her under a microscope for sure now. It was just a matter of time before he found something.

"Samuel will be pleased to see you!" Fargo yelled behind her.

June hesitated at something in his tone, then decided not to look back as she hurried toward her truck.

June slipped quietly into the back of the community-center auditorium. She was a few minutes late, and the audience was already being held rapt by the charismatic man striding across the stage as he spoke—no one even glanced her way as she quietly opened the back door. But Samuel noticed her entrance. He stopped on the stage and smiled, as if right at her.

June felt a little punch to the chest.

She nodded her head and smiled back, hatred filling her body. But she needed to put in an emergency appearance to shore up her cover with Samuel. Her facade had started to slip—the stakes were death.

This was Jesse's fault, she thought as she edged along the crowded back row of the auditorium and took a vacant seat, her heart racing.

"When you become the best you that you can be—" Samuel was saying into his mike "—it can arouse feelings of envy and inadequacy in others who have not yet attained this change for themselves."

He stilled, faced the audience. Silence hung. The audience, almost imperceptibly, leaned forward.

The lights dimmed slightly, while a single spot simultaneously brightened on Samuel. His hair seemed to shine, his shirt turn whiter. His eyes appeared to dance.

He was a true master of subliminal effect, thought June—the bastard.

"We're reformers, all of us here," he said with a wide sweep of his tanned and muscled arm. "We have found a new way of seeing the world. But—" He paused, seeming to meet each Devotee's gaze individually.

"Reformers by their very nature are defined by their adversaries, who feel threatened by the change in status quo—they want to tear down the very houses we build!" His voice rose, and he himself seemed to grow in stature. "They want to break down our community!"

Heads in the audience nodded and there were murmurs of assent.

"And it's appropriate that these adversaries be identified, and the truth of them be told! Our foes are many and they include corrupt and abusive federal officials."

He was referring to the FBI, thought June, Hawk in particular.

Samuel strode smoothly, deliberately, to the other end of the stage, as if pondering something very grave and heavy indeed. "Our foes include corporations, and they include groups who disguise themselves by offering to help Devotees 'escape' the perfection we have created here."

June felt her face warm. She focused intensely on not showing any further outward reaction, but she feared that somehow Samuel had already seen something change in her, even from where he stood.

Don't be ridiculous, June. You're giving him the same power these Devotees have given him.

"These incompetent organizations are filled with even more incompetent individuals who want to tear each and every one of you away from the wonderful thing we have built right here, in Cold Plains, Wyoming! Our home!"

Samuel reached for a bottle of Cold Plains water on the podium. The water seemed to sparkle in the spotlight. He poured a glass, set the bottle down.

"These enemies," he said somberly, "also hide among us, I'm afraid. They could be our neighbors." He watched the audience carefully. "They could wear the guise of friends. They could even be members of our own families. And the closer they are to us—" he held up his hand "—the more dangerous they are to our well-being. We must oust them, each and every one, and they must be cast from our souls and our town!"

June's hands tightened in her lap—he was starting a bloody witch hunt! McCarthyism was going to have nothing on this guy, and she was in his crosshairs.

It was dark and still raining by the time June returned to the cave house in the mountains. She was beat, her emotions simmering far too close to the surface. She hugged Eager tightly and put her face in his fur. His doggie scent, his soft Labrador ears, his delight in seeing her always grounded June.

After she'd showered quickly and changed, she went to the kitchen to feed Eager and prepare a meal for her captive. Guilt gnawed at her.

Before returning to the cave house, June had checked in on Hannah, who seemed to think their cover was still intact. But they were all on edge now. June had also tried to call Hawk Bledsoe, but the FBI agent's voice mail said he was out of town.

June had then driven out to the ranch where Hawk stayed

with his new wife, Carly, and Carly's sister Mia. Carly had informed her that Hawk had flown back to the D.C. field office and would be gone for a few days. She suggested June go to the other FBI agents at their cabin in the woods. But it was Hawk June trusted, and it was his input she wanted. June decided she'd think on it until morning. Until then, Jesse was her responsibility, and it weighed heavily upon her.

She'd heard no rumors in town about a missing male, and after what Lacy had described, and what June had seen on Jesse's GPS, plus the freshness of his tattoo, she was becoming increasingly convinced that he was *not* one of Samuel's men.

Then again, after hearing Samuel's seminar today, June wouldn't put it past him to try to get a mole into their safehouse system. With eleven of his Devotees suddenly missing now, Samuel knew *something* was going down. And June couldn't rule out the possibility Jesse could be Samuel's mole, and that he'd been sent in over the north mountains with a fresh tattoo as some kind of ruse.

Carrying the tray of food and some clean clothes, June took a deep breath as Brad, who'd taken over the guard position from Molly, unlocked the bedroom door for her.

She entered and he locked the door behind her.

Jesse was reclined on the bed, shirt off, and he was reading a book. He glanced up. Nerves bit at her.

He made her room seem small, intimate, warm. He made her feel ridiculously feminine. And the partial nakedness of his body, the casualness with which he relaxed in her space, made her ache suddenly for a once-familiar feeling of having a lover, a partner. Someone, just sometimes, she could lean on. A team. As she'd once, so long ago now, been with Matt.

This vignette, irrespective of who he was or where he'd come from, just drove home how lonely June really was.

"It got a bit hot in here." He closed the book, sat up and swung his legs over the side of the bed. "Some fresh air would be nice."

She cleared her throat and approached the bed. "I brought you some clean clothes and some supper," she said, setting the tray on the table. The neatly folded jeans, socks, shirt and underwear she placed in a pile on the bed beside him. His belt lay atop the pile.

He stared at the buckle—the bronze letters: *Jesse.* A strange look crossed his face.

June dug into her jeans pocket and handed him his watch.

"I took it off when I stitched you up."

He looked up into her eyes, and she felt a jolt of electrical energy.

"So now I'm allowed to know what day it is, even if I can't see daylight?"

June swallowed, still holding the watch out to him. "I'm sorry, Jesse. It's only…for a short while."

"What're you waiting for? The feds to arrive?"

"You really that afraid of law enforcement?"

Slowly, he reached up, took his watch from her hands. His skin brushed hers as he did. His hand was warm, rough, and the touch sent a wave of goose bumps chasing up her arm. Then suddenly, he grabbed her wrist.

And before she could even think, he had her Glock out of her holster with his other hand.

June cursed her stupidity as panic licked through her stomach.

"June," he said quietly as clicked off the safety, his eyes intense, "I don't want to hurt you, but I *need* to get out of here."

Chapter 5

Jesse could see the fear and anger in her eyes—fear he'd put there.

"I should have known better than to trust you." Her voice was hoarse.

He could smell her shampoo—she'd just had a shower, and her hair was drying in loose waves over her shoulders; it looked like it did in the photograph on the dresser. She was wearing a soft blue-and-white-checked flannel shirt over a white T-shirt and her narrow jeans were tucked into Ugg boots. Not an ounce of makeup adorned her finely boned features. Apart from the angry flush in her cheeks now, she looked tired.

Compassion mushroomed softly in his chest.

"I need to go to Cold Plains," he said quietly. "I need to find Samuel Grayson."

She swallowed, her gaze flicking to the gun. "Why?"

"Because it might help me figure out why I came here."

"Maybe you're his mole," she said.

"Why would I be wanting to leave, then?"

She was silent for several beats. "I don't know. Samuel is a sociopathic con artist, a master at mental games. Perhaps he sent you in over the mountains to play one of those mental games with me."

"I don't think so, June."

"Maybe you don't *know* so." Her features were tight. "Maybe your amnesia is genuine—you did get a knock on the head. And you could regain your memory, recall why you're here and then hurt the people I'm trying to save."

Jesse got up suddenly and she tensed. He went to the dresser and put the loaded gun on top, then he put on his watch. He walked over to the chair where she'd set the pile of clothes and pulled a fresh white T-shirt over his head.

"I see you found some jeans my size," he said, taking off his track pants.

Her gaze darted between him and the gun on the dresser as he pulled on the jeans and put on his belt. The anger spots high on her cheekbones darkened and confusion crept into her eyes. Be damned if it didn't make her sexier.

"What're you doing?" she said.

"Getting dressed."

She hesitated, then edged toward the dresser, picked up the gun, turned to face him. "Why'd you do that?"

She was shaking slightly.

"Because I can, June. I wanted to show you that I can overpower you if I want to. I *can* hurt people if I choose to." He faced her squarely. "I wanted to prove to you that even when the situation is in my control, I won't hurt you, or anyone else in this house."

She moistened her lips. He could see conflict in her features, and Jesse had an absurd desire to hold her, comfort her, tell her she should get some rest from saving the world.

"Maybe it's just part of your mind game," she said coolly, holstering her weapon.

"Not going to keep the gun pointed at me?"

"There's a loaded twelve-gauge outside that door." She jerked her chin toward the door. "I just have to scream."

He smiled. "You trust me now, even just a little."

"I don't trust you as far as I could throw you."

"But you'll let me out."

She said nothing.

Jesse inhaled deeply. He had to try another tack.

"How far is it into town?" he said

"A few hours on foot."

"You said you were a part-time paramedic. You spoke about a cult of Devotees and this being a safe house. Did you bring the occupants in here—did you rescue them all from Samuel Grayson's cult?"

"Jesse, I—"

"Please," he said. "*Help* me. The more I know, the more it might jog my memory."

She raked her hands over that gorgeous red hair. She was unsure about him, yet she cared, too. She was a good, strong and fascinating person, clearly with a keen sense of duty that kept a fire burning in her.

"June, you said earlier that you do what you do because of your husband—that's why you wear his ring, as a symbol. Can you tell me about him? What happened?"

She glanced toward the photo on the dresser.

"Is that him in that photo? Is that your son?"

Her eyes flashed to him with such a sudden fierce and crackling energy it took him aback.

"If you need anything else," she said coolly, "just call out to the guard outside." She turned to leave, her shoulders tight, and Jesse saw that her hands were fisted at her sides.

"June, please, talking to me might help me figure out who I am. I—I *need* you to talk to me."

She stilled, her back to him. And she stayed like that for several beats.

Jesse came up behind her and he placed his hand on her shoulder. It was slender, her muscles tight.

"June," he said very softly, turning her around, and he saw tears pooled in her eyes.

"Come," he said, sliding his hand down her arm and taking her hand. "Come sit down." He tried to lead her to the bed.

But she shrugged him off and swiped the tears from her face.

"I'm tired," she said crisply. "That's all."

"Tired of doing what you do?"

"Look, it's been a long day." She reached for the door. "Please, just stay in here tonight. I'll have something worked out by tomorrow."

"What were their names—your husband's and son's?"

She seemed suddenly frozen.

"At least you have your memories, June," he said quietly. "I have nothing but the present."

"That's how *he* does it, you know. Samuel finds the chink, then he pries it open, makes you talk, and then he's got you."

"That's not what I'm doing, June."

"And how would I know?"

He hesitated a beat. "You wouldn't."

She studied him, and he could see the intelligence in her features. He also wanted to kiss her mouth. Damn, he wanted to take her in his arms, do a lot more.

But as the thought occurred to him, he was slammed by an image of a dark-haired woman, screaming, in pain. And in his mind he heard a child crying—terrible cries. And he felt desperate, helpless. Responsible. Then there was just blackness—an awful, aching void of nothing.

The blood drained from his head. He reached up, touched his stitches.

"Are you all right?"

Her gaze shot to her. "I don't know."

She hesitated. "I'll talk to you, Jesse, but only if you eat while I do. You need to eat something. Is that a deal?"

He snorted softly at the power shift. "Deal."

June moved to a chair near the stove and sat. Light from the flames inside flickered like soft copper fire over her hair. She released a big breath of air. "I feel bad enough as it is about locking that door—I suppose I owe you. I just wish I could trust you, that I had some kind of proof you don't belong to Samuel."

"Believe me, I'd like to know, too."

"Case rested for locking you up." But a smile curved her lips when she said it, and Jesse's heart stalled for a nano-second.

"You should do that more often," he said quietly.

"What?"

"Smile."

She flushed, and his blood heated. Jesse seated himself at the small table where she'd placed his food. He picked up the knife and fork. "See? Eating."

"My husband's name was Matt," she said quietly. "Matt Farrow."

"He was a pilot?"

She nodded, hands tight in her lap.

"It's difficult to talk about?"

She nodded again, eyes glimmering, her nose going slightly pink. Then she lurched to her feet.

"It shouldn't be," she snapped and began to pace the room, her long legs sexy as all hell in those jeans. An image of getting those sheepskin boots off her flashed through his mind.

On the back of it came the faceless image of the dark-haired woman. His pulse quickened.

"Why shouldn't it be difficult?"

She spun to face him.

"It's been *five* years, Jesse. Matt and Aiden have been gone that long now. I—I've been fine—dealt with it."

"You're still wearing his ring, June."

"I don't mean that I want to forget him. I mean I thought I'd put the grief into perspective, that I'd gone through the stages. But…I don't know. It's just hurting at the moment. I don't know why."

Jesse set his knife and fork down slowly, a sense of loss filling him, as if June was reminding him of something. He heard the baby screaming again in his memory somewhere. Then he saw an image of a hospital. He felt the guilt again. The name Samuel Grayson began to circle in his head.

"Is the food not good?"

He stared at it—vegetable lasagna and salad. "No, it's great, I…thought I was remembering something, that's all." He glanced up at her.

She assessed him for a beat, then reseated herself beside the stove. "My son's name was Aiden," she said.

"How old was he?" Jesse asked quietly

She inhaled deeply. "Jesse, I really don't want to do this, not with you. I'm beat. This whole thing…this day…no sleep…it's just left everything a little raw. I'm not usually like this."

"*What* whole thing?" he said, a kind of desperation rising in him.

She turned her face away from him, stared at the flames in the little window of the stove.

"Finding you," she said finally. "Finding you has messed everything up. I… Jesus, I'm sorry, Jesse, but my actions, the fact I brought you here instead of going on an official search—it's made my cover thin. It could cost lives. And I don't know what the hell to do with you."

"Cost lives?"

She looked at him. "Samuel is dangerous. He's a murderer. The feds know it but they haven't managed to get enough on him to lay charges and prosecute."

He took a bite of his vegetable lasagna, chewed as he digested what she'd said. And in part of his brain he wondered if she was vegetarian. He liked his meat—venison. He stilled. It was another small snippet of revelation. He had a sudden image of blood, warm on his hands. And then it was gone.

"So you work as a paramedic and a SAR volunteer in Cold Plains," he said. "This is your cover. Meanwhile, in the dark of night, you bring people to this…cave place, whatever it is."

"That pretty much sums it up."

"And you were searching for Lacy and her kids when you stumbled upon me."

She nodded. "I should have been on an official search for Lacy on the other side of the mountain—it's a long story. But I couldn't just leave you down that ravine." She swore. "Now a crooked cop is going to look deeper into me and my background and people I care for are going to get hurt or killed."

"June?"

"What?"

"Thank you. For saving my life."

She raised her arms as if in defeat. "And where does that get me—us—now?"

"Maybe I can help you."

Surprise darted through her eyes. Then she said, very quietly, "Jesse, you could still be a mole."

He scooped up the last mouthful of lasagna and chewed, watching her.

"Tell me about Matt," he said.

She slumped back in her chair.

"He was a helicopter pilot who flew SAR missions. It's how I met him, on a search. We married young. Well, I was young. He was quite a bit older than me, and we had Aiden. We were good together." She sat silent awhile. "PTSD is a little-acknowledged fact of SAR life, and there always comes one mission that gets to you for some reason. That day came for Matt, a seasoned veteran, when he was called out to look for another chopper that had gone down in the Cascades. The search turned into a recovery mission. The craft had crashed into the side of a mountain in heavy weather. No survivors. The pilot was a close friend of Matt's—brothers-in-arms kind of thing. And it was a pretty gruesome recovery effort. It cut Matt up big-time."

She sighed deeply. "And it left him questioning the meaning of it all, life. One of his friends suggested Matt go with him to a church meeting. That meeting led to another, and then another, and pretty soon, he was sucked in by a religious cult." Her eyes narrowed and Jesse could see she was struggling.

"It wasn't like Matt was weak," she said. "But what I just didn't get at the time is that you don't have to be somehow weak or stupid to be sucked in by a cult. And there was my guy—an über A-type personality, a total daredevil who was so in control and command of his own environment—being sucked in by the ministerings of some cult leader."

"What did you do?"

She snorted. "I tried to talk sense into him. Then we argued. The arguments got worse. Then I went to some meetings in an effort to see what in hell he was talking about. And—" she shook her head. "I still didn't get why my intelligent guy couldn't just snap out of it. But that's not how it works, I've learned. And then the church wanted money. Matt was starting to dig into our savings, giving everything we'd worked for together to the cult. I'd lost him, Jesse. He spent more and more time away from home. And I began to worry about Aiden. He was only three years old at the time, and Matt started taking him to the church meetings. And when Matt started talking about us all moving onto the church's rural compound in the mountains, I drew my line in the sand. I told him he had to choose between our marriage and the cult, because he was bleeding us dry."

June rubbed her face. "I thought—I honestly believed, at the time—that it was a matter of making a decision, that Matt was strong, and that he would make the right choice. But that evening I was called out on a missing Alzheimer's case. I took Aiden to my mom's house and she promised to get him to day care in the morning.

"When I went to pick him up the following evening, they told me Matt had come earlier in the day and taken him. I knew right away he was taking him to the cult compound. I called the cops. It turned into a huge manhunt. Matt went into the woods. I used the dog I had at the time, tried to track them." Her eyes began to gleam with emotion.

"I tracked the whole night."

She sat silent awhile.

Jesse pushed his plate aside.

"What happened?" he said, his voice hoarse.

She snorted softly. "Matt reached a helicopter base in the next town and he took Aiden with him in one of their choppers. The police took a helicopter up, followed him. I—I knew he wouldn't have taken Aiden up with him unless he was totally desperate, not thinking. Otherwise he'd have known there was a finite amount of fuel, that he'd have to set down, that the police would pick him up when he did."

"He crashed?"

She nodded.

Wood popped in the fire.

"I'm so sorry," he said. He felt lame.

"I learned a lesson that day, Jesse. A brutal lesson about the psychological power of cults. I learned that you can't just snap out of it, that you need professional help to do so. If I'd gone about it a different way, found counseling, helped Matt deal with the real reasons he'd gone to the church in the first place... Because, in retrospect, he was suffering from critical-incident stress. I didn't see it, and he certainly was too macho to talk to me about what was going on deep in his head. I loved him, and I should have found a way to help him. Instead, I gave him an ultimatum that pushed him over the edge. I killed him and my son."

"June—"

She raised her palm and shook her head. "It *is* my fault. I don't care what people say."

"So now you help others out of cults, and you do it in memory of Matt and Aiden." *Or do you do it to try and assuage your own feelings of guilt—is it the only thing you* can *do now, June?*

She nodded. "I learned everything I could after that. And I started working for EXIT, an international network of like-minded professionals and volunteers who help families get loved ones out of cults and into halfway houses, safe places, where they can access deprogramming or exit-counseling. I move around the country, operating safe houses where necessary."

"And that's how you came to Cold Plains?"

"Yes."

"Who brought you here—I mean, which family?"

"In this case the existence of the Devotees came to EXIT's attention via one of the escapees, Mia Finn, who was brought in for deprogramming. She's now the sister-in-law of the FBI agent investigating Samuel. Samuel's believed to be responsible for orchestrating the murders of at least five women and possibly others."

"This is dangerous."

"That's an understatement."

Jesse's respect, his attraction to June, mushroomed.

"I can't believe I'd be working for a guy like Samuel," he said.

"Yet you mentioned his name. You said you had something urgent to do. You have a tattoo."

He inhaled deeply. "I'm obviously here in connection with Samuel, or the town. That's why you need to unlock that door for me, June, let me go and find out why I'm here."

"Let me sleep on it, Jesse. You need sleep, too." She got up and made for the door.

He got up and grasped her wrist. "June—"

She turned. She was so close. And he could see the rawness of the emotion glimmering in her eyes, in the slight pinkness of her nose. Her eyes darkened and he could see physical attraction. The notion hung suddenly, tangible between them.

Fire crackled and popped softly in the stove.

"What?" she whispered, her voice thick, and Jesse was suddenly unable to tear his attention from her lips, the way her breathing was making her chest rise and fall. And before he could even think to finish his sentence, he leaned in and he kissed her mouth.

She jerked back, eyes wide in shock.

But before she could say a word, a loud banging sounded on the bedroom door.

June spun around just as the door was flung open by Brad, shotgun in his hand, his face white.

Sonya was right behind him, her eyes bright with fear, a radio in her hand. Molly was at her side. She pointed straight at Jesse, arm outstretched.

"It's his fault!" yelled Molly. "He brought them here!"

"*What's* his fault?" said June. "What's going on?"

"Davis just called in," Sonya said. "A posse of five henchmen is approaching the rock crevasse that leads to the tunnel. He could hear them talking. He thinks they said something about a mole in the safe house."

"See?" yelled Molly, borderline hysterical. "You shouldn't have brought him here. He's leading them in somehow."

June shot a glance at Jesse

He was tense, eyes narrowed and hard as he stared at Molly.

"It's not possible," June said. "Jesse has no way of contacting—"

Davis's voice crackled suddenly through the radio in Sonya's hand. June took it from her, stepping out into the passageway. Brad started to close the bedroom door.

Jesse placed his hand on the door, stopping it from closing. "June, let me help," he said.

"Are you crazy? It's your fault they're here!" Molly kicked the bedroom door closed in his face, and he heard the key turning in the lock.

His muscles strapped tight in a band across his chest. He jiggled the handle. Locked.

Cursing, he swung around, glared at the windowless rock walls, listening to the sound of urgent talking fade down the passage. He raked his hand angrily over his hair, frustration burning through his blood, and he swore again. He felt as though he'd entered some kind of surreal universe, being trapped in a cave room by a woman and a motley assortment of kids and adults with guns.

He could break down the door, do something rash, which was what he was pumping to do right now, but he had little doubt that that trigger-happy Molly kid would blow him apart with that twelve-gauge before he was out.

Maybe henchmen arriving would be a good thing.

* * *

There was better reception in the kitchen where the radio could pick up waves through the windows from the portable repeater June had rigged up outside.

"June to Davis. Can you repeat? What's going on?" June released the key, tension winding tight in the kitchen. She glanced at the others gathered around her.

The radio crackled to life. "Davis to safe house. Five armed henchmen combing the woods." He spoke quietly, as if he wasn't far from the men.

"They came close to the crevasse entrance but veered south before discovering it. I followed them for about two miles. They're actively searching for something with hunting spots—all are armed. Are you getting this, June?"

"Loud and clear. Go on, Davis," June said, releasing the key again.

"I heard one say something about a mole on the inside and that they were waiting for the mole to make contact."

Ice shot down June's spine. She keyed the radio.

"Are you sure?"

"That's what it sounded like. Over."

"Are they still moving south, away from the tunnel entrance?"

"Yes."

"Go back and guard the tunnel entrance, Davis. I'll send someone to relieve you in an hour. Copy?"

"Copy."

Molly's eyes were huge. "Do you want me to go relieve him? I'll go now."

"You need sleep," June said crisply.

"*Sleep*—are you crazy? With them out there?" She flung her arm out in the direction of the hill.

"It's Brad's turn next." June's tone brooked no argument. Molly scowled and stomped out of the kitchen.

June slumped onto a stool at the kitchen counter, heart pounding.

Maybe Jesse really is a mole.

The memory of his kiss filled her mind. She thought of the compassion she'd seen in his eyes and sensed in his touch. He *felt* like a good man. Or was she being completely blinded by her physical attraction to him? Was seducing her a part of his game?

June scrubbed her hands over her face, wondering when this job had gotten so damn complicated. She wished Hawk Bledsoe would return. She wanted him to nail Samuel and for this whole thing to be over, because she was wearing dangerously thin.

Chapter 6

It was morning, early. The rain had stopped and the sun was painting the world that beautiful gold that comes when the angle of the sun is still low. June put on a pot of coffee, feeling exhausted. She'd taken one of the beds in the nursery where Lacy and the twins were sleeping, but she'd lain wide-awake listening to the others breathe, thinking how different the rhythm of a child's breathing was from an adult's, how close this mother and her babies had come to losing their lives.

Were they alive now because of Jesse?

June had also mulled over what Davis had told her when he'd returned to the cave house later in the night. Instead of going back to guard the canyon entrance as June had instructed, Davis had taken it upon himself to follow the posse of henchmen deeper into the woods as they'd beat the bush and panned hunting lights through the trees.

"I definitely heard them say the word *mole*," he'd told June.

"But it wasn't clear that this mole was inside our safe house?" she'd asked.

"No. At first I assumed they meant the mole was in the safe house, and I figured immediately that the mole was Jesse, but as I followed them farther it became blatantly clear that they're no friends of our stranger—they were hunting him. I heard one say Samuel wanted him dead or alive."

"They referred to him by name?" June said.

"No—they don't know who he is."

So he isn't working for Samuel.

Adrenaline trilled through June.

"One of them said the stranger shot Jason Barnes. And, June, I heard them say Barnes died from his wound earlier today."

Jesse had killed him. June cursed softly. Samuel was not going to let this slide. This whole town was going to blow. "Did you recognize the guys in the posse?" she said quietly.

"Rufus Kittridge was leading the group."

"The *mayor?* Are you serious?"

"Lumpy Smithers was there, too. And Monica Pearl. I saw both their faces when they were momentarily illuminated by the hunting spots, but I didn't get a good look at the others." Davis shook his head as if in disbelief. "Who'd have thought Monica Pearl was one of Samuel's enforcers. She's so…sweet."

And pretty, thought June. That was the danger of Samuel Grayson and his cult. The more clean, friendly, benign the facade—the more sinister what lurked beneath.

"Just before I left them, I heard Mayor Kittridge yelling at Lumpy that he should've gotten a better look at the stranger's face. Lumpy argued it was dark, raining and that Jason was badly injured. Rufus hit back that Samuel maintained Lumpy should have gone after the Matthews woman and her kids instead of trying to save Jason. I swear, June, they were wire-tense, really going at each other. Lumpy sounded real choked about Jason dying."

Davis had also returned with a small, muddy pacifier that he'd found while following the men.

"Maybe it belongs to Dr. Black's baby?" he said.

Dr. Rafe Black's infant son had been kidnapped last month and so far there'd been no leads, no ransom notes, nothing—Rafe was devastated. June made a mental note to go search the area around where the pacifier had been found. Rafe Black was a good man, and he was not a Devotee.

Once the coffee was ready, June poured a mug and set it on a tray along with a toasted bagel for Jesse. Outside the bedroom door she waited while Sonya unlocked it.

"Morning," he said as the door opened. "I take it we weren't invaded last night. Too bad. The enemy might have sprung me."

"They didn't find the tunnel," she said as she set the tray on the table. He'd just showered—his hair was damp. He was wearing jeans, his engraved belt and a button-down denim shirt over a white T-shirt—he looked all Wyoming cowboy, and it was a look that really did it for June.

"I'm sorry about last night," he said quietly.

She glanced at him and knew instantly he was talking about the kiss. Her pulse quickened and her mouth felt dry. All she could think about suddenly was how she'd wanted to kiss him back. Instead, she looked away and fiddled unnecessarily with the napkin on the tray. "It's me who should be apologizing," she said quietly. "For locking you up. But I had to be sure that you weren't the mole who'd brought the henchmen so close last night."

She looked up at him and her heart kicked. He exuded a new kind of energy this morning. Sleep had restored him.

And his eyes crackled with an intensity of focus that made her feel hot inside.

"Either way, you are the reason they came looking, Jesse," she said. "When Davis returned he told me the men were armed and actively hunting you. But it seems no one saw your face the other night and they don't know who you are."

A quiet electricity seemed to ripple through his body. "I'm not sure whether I should be pleased or disappointed," he said.

"It appears you killed one of them, Jesse. A man named Jason Barnes died of a gunshot wound to the neck."

Silence filled the room.

"Jesus," he said softly.

"Samuel is after your blood." She inhaled deeply. "Obviously you don't work for him. I'm really sorry I locked you up. I—I've never done anything like this in my life. It's just—things got desperate."

His gaze went to the door.

"It's not locked. You're free to go."

His attention shifted back to her, eyes intense. He stood slowly and took a step toward her. June's knees felt weak.

"Don't go into Cold Plains, Jesse, please—they'll kill you."

"You said they hadn't seen my face."

"You can't just show up in a town like Cold Plains with stitches on your head and no belongings. They'll instantly peg you for the man they were hunting."

"June, I—"

"*Please,* it could endanger us all."

He studied her intently. "Show me around the house," he said, something dark entering his voice.

A whisper of trepidation feathered over her. "You don't want your breakfast?"

"Not in here. But after a tour of the house I'd love a cup of coffee, if you'll share one with me."

She smiled. "You make it sound like a date."

His eyes held hers for several beats. "June, I am sorry—about the kiss."

"I'm not," she said very quietly, her cheeks warming.

But even as she said the words, she realized the stupidity of them—she was physically attracted to, and quite possibly falling for, a man she didn't know at all. He could have loved ones waiting for him to return, worrying about him. There might be no room in his life for someone like her.

June turned and walked to the door, telling herself she didn't want there to be room for her, anyway—she had a life mission. Falling for a stranger who might wake up and realize he belonged to someone else would break her heart. It was ridiculous even to be thinking like this.

She opened the door and strode briskly down the passage. "Kitchen and main living area are this way," she said coolly.

Jesse entered the living space behind June. A fire burned in a big stone hearth, next to which sat a gaunt, hook-nosed, middle-aged man with wary eyes. He was drinking from a pottery mug. Eager was curled at his feet. The man nodded at Jesse. Eager's tale gave a small thump.

"Morning," the man said.

"This is Davis," June said. "He's the one who followed the hunting party last night."

Davis got up, and Jesse stepped forward to shake his hand. Davis had a firm, wiry grasp. Jesse put him in his fifties, and his eyes were not friendly.

"Those guys want your head, mate, whoever you are," he said to Jesse.

Jesse snorted. "Thanks for bringing back the information. Got me out of the bedroom."

Davis, however, wasn't going to let Jesse off that easy.

"No one knows we have a safe house out in this valley," he

said coolly. "Those henchmen were not looking for a secret crevasse or a tunnel or a cave house. They were looking for you—*you* brought them out onto the west flank. We're just lucky they didn't stumble onto the tunnel. Because if they find it—people are going to die."

"I'm sorry." Jesse didn't know what else to say, and he judged it imprudent to point out that henchmen had already, apparently, been on the west flank searching for Lacy Matthews and her daughters.

Davis reached for his gun. "I'm going to relieve Tiffany, who's out there with a radio right now, watching. But we're not militia. We're not trained for this. We're just ordinary folk who want to get safely the hell out of Cold Plains now."

"We'll have you all moved out of here within the next few days," June told Davis. "That hunting posse didn't find any sign of Jesse. I don't think they're going to come back this way in a hurry."

Davis grunted and left.

"Do you believe that, June?" Jesse said, watching Davis go.

"That they won't be back for a while?" She sighed deeply. "I hope they won't. Because Davis is right. We're not equipped for this.

"This is the kitchen." June stepped into a beam of sunlight streaming down from skylights above and sun flamed like fire on her hair, stalling Jesse's thoughts entirely. And in that instant he wondered if he'd ever come across a more enigmatic or beautiful woman. He liked everything about her— her grace of movement, her strength. Her surety of vision. Her courage. He loved the way she looked. And when she turned to face him in the kitchen—dear God—those clear, summer-sky eyes.

His chest clutched and desire welled sharp and sudden in him, along with a raw urge to make her smile. He wanted to hear her laugh, see the light dance in those eyes. Bottom line, Jesse had an urge to protect her, to help her with this burden she'd undertaken.

Was that the kind of person he was? Or was it his lust speaking?

"Everything in here is run off solar power," she said.

Jesse turned to study the kitchen—the wood cabinetry was high-end, the countertops granite. The windows at the far end of the room were tinted and large and looked out onto a valley of low scrub and pockets of trees. Light fittings were crafted from wrought iron or bone—shades made from what looked like hide. In fact, everything about the place seemed rustic high-end, artistic and wilderness-inspired.

"What is this place?" he said. "It's incredible."

"It was built into the caves by a manic-depressive architect who decided to go survivalist and live off the grid, but in style. There are more rooms this way," she said, holding out her arm.

June led him down another stone passageway into a room that had been equipped as a nursery.

Lacy and her twins were sitting on one of the beds. Lacy had a book in her hands and was reading her girls a story. She glanced up sharply as they entered. The twins seemed to sense tension in their mother and instinctively cuddled closer.

Jesse stilled in the doorway, struck by the vignette. The children were brunettes, like their mother, and identical. And he knew one thing about himself with abrupt certainty: if someone tried to kill this young mother and her children again—he'd shoot the bastard dead.

What did that say about him?

"Hello," he said to the girls, his voice coming out too deep. "My name is—" He glanced at June. "They call me Jesse."

"You're the bad man," said one of the twins

"I...don't think so."

The kids stared at him.

Jesse suddenly felt hot, and a dark cesspool of guilt swirled inside him. With it came twinges of rage, remorse, hurt. A cool sense of betrayal.

He shook himself, wanting to bury the uncomfortable sensations but knowing on some level they were parts of his memory coming closer to the surface of his consciousness, like tiny agitating bubbles in a pot of water ready to break into a boil and release steam. And it scared him to think what lurked down there.

June touched his arm, jolting him back to the present.

"The other rooms are this way."

"It's a big place," he said as she showed him a series of bedrooms, bathrooms and a games room complete with billiard table.

She nodded. "When the architect died, he left everything to his sister, who lives in the town over. She didn't know what to do with the place. It's not legal, no building permits, and there is no road access. Then her sister-in-law, Hannah Mendes, needed a safe house. It was the perfect solution. We heard about Hannah from Mia Finn during her deprogramming sessions. That's where I came in. Hannah is in her seventies, works at the Cold Plains water-bottling warehouse, and she identifies vulnerable cultees and gets them out. They come here, then go into an exit-counseling program." June showed him into a hallway that led to what appeared to be the front door.

Jesse noted a gun rack mounted near the door. A shotgun rested on the wood slats. Beside the rack was a cabinet that held ammunition. The key to the cabinet was in the lock. He saw there were boxes of both shells and slugs in the cabinet.

His gaze shifted down to June's hips, to the Glock in her holster.

She opened a heavy oak door and he followed her out onto

a stone patio covered partially by a rock overhang. The morning sun was warming the valley and the vegetation smelled like summer. A sense of familiarity washed over him, and he was gripped by a powerful notion that he belonged outdoors, that he slept often under the stars. That he needed to roam the mountains. On the back of that thought rode the dark, cold feelings of guilt again. Jesse began to itch with irritability, impatient to get deeper inside his head, find the answers.

"This is Hidden Valley," June said. She was standing next to him, and he could smell her shampoo again. Eager was at her feet, sunlight glinting off his black fur. Jesse walked to the end of the patio where a small creek burbled, the sun warm on his shoulders. It was a calm place, a healing place, he thought.

"How did this architect bring in the building materials for the house?" he said.

"Chopper. He had a pilot friend. He also had wealth."

Jesse whistled softly. "It's a perfect place to hide." He turned to June. "You said you move people from here into exit-counseling. How do the safe-house occupants get out of the valley from here?"

"We have to hike out that way, to the next town." She nodded to the mountains. "It's a fair trek, takes several hours. I've learned exit-counseling myself, so I start that right away. There's a town called Little Gulch on the other side of that mountain. EXIT has stationed a psychologist there who handles counseling and helps with transitions."

Jesse put his hand to his temple and felt the line of stitches. His head was beginning to hurt.

"You okay?"

"I… The idea of needing to get someone into deprogramming feels familiar somehow."

He saw a flicker of nervousness in her eyes. "Maybe you came here trying to get someone out, Jesse. Could you have been thinking of faking your way in with a false Devotee tattoo?"

He frowned, the image of a slight, dark-haired woman curling into his mind again. He felt himself fiddling with his ring finger and a wave of nausea hit him.

"I have no idea," he said quietly. The woman in his mind began to scream again. And this time he saw flames. He felt the heat of fire, heard it crackling, consuming, swallowing her. His mouth felt dry. He wanted June to shut up.

June saw a haunted look creeping into Jesse's eyes and the despair in his features made her chest tighten. She couldn't help it—she reached out, placed her hand on his arm.

"Hey," she said. "It's going to be okay. It'll come back to you."

"Maybe I don't want it to," he whispered. "Maybe I am some kind of bad guy, June. Maybe I've done something terrible."

And again that little whisper of doubt curled through her.

"Jesse—"

But before the next word could come out of her mouth, screaming came from the bushes.

They both spun around to see Brad crashing out from the brush, his eyes wide with fear. Eager began to bark excitedly as Brad ran toward the patio yelling. "Help! Molly's in trouble!"

Adrenaline punched through June. *The henchmen—they must be here!*

She rushed indoors, grabbed the shotgun from the rack and hurriedly unlocked the cabinet, reaching for a box of shells.

Brad reached the patio and bent over, bracing his hands on his knees as he tried to catch his breath. "Bears!" he said. "Molly's trapped by a mother bear and her cubs."

June froze, gun in hand. *"Bears?"*

Brad stood up. His face glistened with sweat. "They have Molly cornered at that end of the valley." He pointed toward the mountains.

"She said she was going to pick some berries. I followed her—I wanted to see where the berries were. But there's a big bear and her cubs stalking her."

June began to load the gun. Jesse placed his hand on her arm, stopping her.

She shot him a glance.

His eyes were narrowed. "Give it to me," he said, grabbing the gun from her with force.

Shock licked through June. "No, Jesse! What the—"

He turned away from her and went back inside. She rushed after him, anger spearing into her.

"What do you think you're doing? Give that back to me—Molly's in trouble."

He reached into the cabinet and took out a box of slugs. He reloaded the gun.

"Buckshot is useless against a charging bear," he said, quickly loading the gun. He clicked it in place. "You need slugs. Even so, you have to hit just right or you're dead."

She stared, dumbfounded.

"Come," he said. Then he nodded at Brad. "You, too. We stick together in a group—it'll make us look big to the bears. Follow my lead, and whatever you do, don't run. Which way is she? Show me," he said to Brad.

Brad led them to a narrow trail through the low scrub.

Jesse began to hike into the bush.

"Wait!" June quickly grabbed Eager's collar and took him back to the house. "I'm taking him back. I don't want him to get hurt," she said.

"Catch up to us, then," Jesse called over his shoulder.

June ran back to the cave house with Eager and yelled for Sonya to look after him.

"How do you know this stuff about bears?" June said, breathless, when she caught up to Jesse and Brad.

"I don't know. I just do."

June struggled to keep up with Jesse. He moved with ease and stealth through the wilderness, like a great big mountain lion, all powerful muscle. Brad was panting heavily behind her, crashing through brush clumsily.

They crested a ridge. The sun was warm on their backs.

Jesse pointed. "There they are."

There was a reverence in his voice that made June look up at him. He was squinting into the sunlight and crinkles fanned out from his eyes. He looked rugged—a real Marlboro mountain man, as if he belonged out here, and June felt safe with him.

She'd always been confident on her own in the wilderness. She knew how to navigate, she'd done her survival courses, she knew her firearms, but this sense of security she felt standing beside Jesse was something different. It was like having someone at your side, someone you could lean on if the going got rough, someone who'd take a few knocks and fight off the bad guys for you—as he'd done for Lacy and her daughters.

And June realized again how deeply she missed Matt and being part of a team.

The bears—a sow and her two cubs, their coats reddish-brown—were grazing along a flat part of the valley. They were beautiful, majestic.

"They're healthy," June whispered. "It's not common to see them here. She must've brought her cubs down along the spine of the mountain range."

"This way," said Jesse as he began to walk along the crest of the ridge.

"We're going to approach them head-on?" asked Brad, clearly terrified.

"I want them to see us, to pick up our scent in the wind," Jesse said. "That way they'll most likely just move away."

As he spoke, the mother lifted her nose and tasted the wind.

"There." Jesse smiled. "She got us."

The sow stared in their direction for a while.

"Definitely black bear," June said.

"But they're brown," said Brad

"Black bear can be anything from a soft cinnamon color to pitch-black," Jesse said. "You can tell they're not grizzlies from the shape of their heads and the sow's shoulders. She has no hump."

"So they're not as dangerous?" said Brad.

"Black bears are responsible for more predatory attacks on humans than grizzlies are. You need to respect their space just the same."

"Jesse," June said softly. "Have you seen grizzlies in the wild?"

He nodded. Then turned suddenly to her. Sunlight danced in his eyes, and a smile curved his lips. "I recall being on a horse, in mountains, and seeing bears—brown bears. Not just once. I...feel like it's a part of me."

"You don't get brown bears in this part of Wyoming," she said. "If you've seen them in this state, it's in the northwest. Maybe the Wind River range, Yellowstone, Grand Tetons."

He closed his eyes a moment.

"And I can feel forest, snowcapped peaks, shale slopes. Being out for days at a time."

As he spoke, June saw relief in his features. He liked what he was seeing.

"See?" She grinned, infected by his sudden good energy. "I told you it would start coming back."

"I see Molly!" Brad interrupted. "Over there—look. She's trapped behind the bears and can't get back on the trail."

June saw a figure moving through the scrub a distance behind the bruins.

"She's downwind of them. They don't know she's there," Jesse said. "Come, we need to crowd them a bit, get them to move eastward, away from her."

He began to hike down the ridge, toward the bears, June and Brad following quietly behind. The sow reared up on her hind legs, waving her head back and forth, mouth open.

"She's going to attack," whispered Brad.

"She's just getting a better look, tasting the air," Jesse said.

The bear dropped back onto all fours and began to lumber, slowly, out of the valley, making her way east. The cubs followed.

Molly hugged June, breathless with relief to see them, but Jesse noted she had no basket, no berries.

He walked behind the three of them on the return to the cave house and more memories washed over him. This time he felt himself riding a horse again, with a packhorse tethered to his saddle. He had everything he needed for an extended stay in the mountains—his 270 Winchester rifle at his side and his twelve-gauge Remington WingMaster shotgun. His Beretta was holstered at his hip.

And in his memory he was looking for something... *poachers.* Jesse stopped dead in his tracks, pulse racing, perspiration breaking out over his body. He tried to dig deeper, but the images were gone.

Slowly he began to walk behind June, Brad and Molly again. Molly dropped something—it looked like a cell phone. She quickly scooped it up and glanced behind her to see if Jesse had seen. He looked away, pretending he hadn't.

When they reached the house, Molly and Brad went inside,

but June lingered outside in the sunshine. Jesse was pleased. He liked to watch the way the sun burned fire into her red hair. Her cheeks were pink from the walk and he realized how tired and pale she'd been looking—she still looked tired, but the color in her face stirred something deep in Jesse. He wanted to help her rest, find peace. He wanted to see her smile again.

He held out the shotgun to her.

"Keep it," she said. "I trust you."

Her words sent a warm rush through his chest. June made him feel good. She chased away the darker sensations lingering just under his consciousness, and Jesse realized he was falling, hard, for this woman. It worried him.

Would he be falling for June in the same way if he knew who he was?

She placed her hands on the banister that ran around the edge of the patio overlooking the creek. "Those bears were beautiful, Jesse. It was like a gift seeing them." She paused, looked up at him. "Thank you," she said quietly. "For a moment back there I thought you were going to take the twelve-gauge and split. You didn't have to help Molly." She laughed. "She hasn't exactly been endearing herself to you."

He came up to her, stood closer than he needed to.

"June, do you get cell reception out here?"

"Why?" she said, her features instantly guarded again.

"Just curious."

"We're out of cell-tower range in this valley. There's no reception on the west flank of the mountain on the Cold Plains side, either."

"What about over there?" He nodded in the direction they'd found Molly.

"I don't know," June said. "I haven't tried out there."

"You said there's a town over that far ridge?"

"Yes, Little Gulch. That's where we have an EXIT counselor who handles the transitions from the safe house."

"So, conceivably there might be some cell reception from a tower on the Little Gulch side."

"Like I said, I haven't tried to use a cell phone out there, but I suppose it's feasible."

"How do you get radio reception in the house?"

"Why all the questions?" He heard the suspicion in her tone.

He smiled. "I'm just interested. Radio reception is sketchy even in a parking garage. A cave can't be any better."

Her shoulders relaxed a little. "I rigged up some portable repeaters, same kind as we use for SAR work in remote areas. But there's always a worry one of the Devotee henchmen will stumble upon our radio frequency, so we limit communication to emergencies. Parking garages, huh?"

"Don't ask me how I know."

Her smile deepened.

And Jesse didn't even think about what he did next. He put his arm around June and drew her close. She stiffened for a moment and looked up at him in surprise. Then she looked out over the sunny valley and allowed herself to lean into him. Jesse could feel the tension draining from her muscles as she did. He rested his cheek against her hair. It was warm from the sun, and soft. An ache began in his chest.

"You fit me," he said quietly. "As if you belong."

She said nothing, and when he glanced down at her face her saw the glisten of tears on her cheeks.

"June—"

She shook her head. "It's nothing. I—I've just missed being held."

They stood like that in silence for a while, and more than anything Jesse wanted his memory back, to know who he was. Because he wanted June in his life—he *needed* to know it was possible.

"I have to go to Cold Plains, June," he said. "I need to lay my eyes on this Samuel Grayson, see if it jogs my memory free."

"They'll kill you. We've had this discussion."

"I can't just do nothing."

She pulled out of his embrace.

"Wait for the FBI, Jesse. I trust Agent Hawk Bledsoe. He's away right now, but—"

"No feds."

She swallowed, and concern filtered into her eyes. "Are you really so worried the FBI is going to find something on you, lock you up?"

He didn't answer for a few beats. Worry deepened in her features.

"I told you, I believe there *is* something dark in my past." He paused, trying to figure out how best to articulate his feelings. "Thing is, June, if I've done something illegal, I'll buck up and take the knocks, but I want to know what I've done and why I did it. I want to understand my guilt, my motivations. I don't want to be locked up and just told I've committed some act. I'd prefer to atone for my deeds by choice, in my heart. Does that make any sense at all?"

She was staring at him, a strange look on her face. "Jesse, going to Cold Plains and getting killed is not going to help whatever is haunting you."

He inhaled deeply. "The reason I came here, I believe, is *because* of what is haunting me, June. I've got nothing to lose—"

"Apart from your life!" she snapped.

"But," he said quietly, his gaze holding hers, "I could have everything to gain."

Her heart was thudding hard—he could see it in the pulse at her neck.

"Don't do it, Jesse—don't go."

He grasped her shoulders. "If anything, my leaving will take the heat off you guys here," he said. "If I stay in the house, those men might come back looking for me. You heard Davis. Next time they might find that tunnel."

"Hawk Bledsoe will be back in two days—"

He shook his head. "I'm leaving, June. I won't be here when he arrives."

She stared at him in silence. He became conscious of the chuckling creek, a soft breeze rustling the reeds that grew nearby, the sound of birds.

"I have an idea," she said very quietly. "A plan."

"What kind of plan?"

"It could work, on more than one level—but if it doesn't, we're both dead."

Chapter 7

"It'll be risky," June said as she outlined her plan.

They were sharing breakfast at a small stone table outside, near the water and partially shaded by the rock overhang. From their vantage point they had a full view of the valley and would be able to see anyone approaching. Even as they enjoyed each other's company, they remained watchful.

Eager was lying at June's feet, a warning system himself as he listened to their environment.

"But if you hike out of Hidden Valley that way—" she pointed in the direction Molly had gone earlier "—you reach Little Gulch in about four hours. It's a slightly bigger town than Cold Plains, maybe three thousand residents, and it has a small airstrip. I'll give you a pack and supplies, and you've got GPS." She hesitated. "And I'm going to let you take Eager."

He set his coffee mug down. "Why?"

"Because it will bolster the story I gave the Cold Plains

police chief, Bo Fargo." She rubbed her brow. "I told him the reason for my absence was that Eager got bitten by something, and that I'd taken him to stay overnight at the vet's in Little Gulch because I've had clashes of opinion with the Cold Plains vet—something I need to mend now. So, if I hike back into Cold Plains and pick up my truck, I can—"

"Truck?"

"I live a double life, Jesse. It's complicated. I rent a place on Hannah Mendes's ranch on the outskirts of town. Hannah covers for me all the nights and some days that I am here at the safe house. And I work two days a week for the Cold Plains Urgent Care Center's ambulance service as a paramedic, so I need to put in appearances for that. The job is what allegedly brought me to Cold Plains."

"Plus there's your volunteer SAR work."

She nodded. "And there've been a fair number of searches these days for which they called me because I'm the only volunteer with a validated K9."

"You can't keep this up, June. You've got to find a way to slow down."

"There's no way out now, Jesse. Only one way to go and that's to the end." She took a sip of her coffee. "Once I've got my truck, I'll drive around the mountains to Little Gulch, allegedly to fetch Eager from the vet. I'll make sure someone sees me heading out of town without Eager, and I'll make it known that I'm going to pick him up. Meanwhile, when you get to Little Gulch, go wait for me at a place called Dixon's Pub and Beer Garden. It's a bit of a dive, but it's dog-friendly and it's right on the outskirts of town—it'll be one of the first places you see, big pink neon sign, can't miss it. I'll meet you there later this afternoon."

She took another sip from her mug, and Jesse noticed her hands were shaking slightly.

"June, you really need to rest. You'll—"

"I'm fine," she said briskly. "Tonight is the annual Cold Plains corn-roast festival. We'll drive back into Cold Plains, right down Main Street, while everyone is gathering outside the community center for the festivities. If they see us coming in from the outside, with Eager this time, and if no one recognizes you, I'll tell them that I picked you up from the airstrip when I went to fetch Eager from the vet. You're Hannah's new help for her ranch."

He smiled. "Hope there's a cowboy hat in it for me."

Her eyes remained serious. "Davis has one. You'll need to hide that cut on your head, anyway. Remind me to give you back the cash Sonya found in your jeans pocket before she tossed them."

"She tossed my jeans?"

"I cut the leg open, remember, to see where you were bleeding?"

"And there was nothing else in the pockets?"

"Just a hundred bucks in notes."

He frowned, wondering why he'd had absolutely no identification on him at all.

"If all goes smoothly, we'll mingle awhile at the corn roast. I'll tell everyone we used to date way back, and that I recommended you for the job on Hannah's ranch because you're out of work." Her cheeks pinked a little, and Jesse loved the way her complexion revealed her moods. She probably hated it.

"You better look after Eager—that dog is everything to me."

June was giving him her complete trust, and the scope of what she was trying to achieve struck him square in the chest.

God, he could love this woman, and the thought just fueled his desperation to get out there and find out who he was.

"If we can pull it off tonight, then you can use the work on Hannah's ranch as a cover while you figure things out.

Hannah will pay you for anything you do on the ranch, of course."

"I don't want her money."

"You have a hundred bucks to your name, Jesse. That's it."

"Maybe I'm rich." He grinned. "But I just don't remember."

This time she did smile.

"Yeah, and maybe I'm the Queen of Sheba."

He laughed. Then sobered almost as quickly. "You're right, June, it is risky. Because if someone does recognize me, *you* go down with me. I don't want to take that chance."

"If it works, Jesse, it shores up my story about my absence. It gives Hannah added protection, and you can help us, hiding in plain sight."

"I don't know, June."

She leaned forward. "It's the *only* way you're going to get into Cold Plains alive, Jesse, and God knows Hannah and I could use someone on our team. Besides, if I don't do something to bolster my story with Bo Fargo, stat, he's going to look into it, and I'm going down, anyway. So, do we have a deal?"

Her gaze was direct. Adrenaline rippled through him.

"Deal," he said quietly. "With one caveat. If I think you're going to get hurt, I pull the plug." As Jesse spoke, he caught sight of Molly watching them from behind the window.

"And one more thing—we don't tell anyone in the safe house what we're about to do," he said, his eye on Molly.

"Because?"

"Because they're safe in what they don't know."

June trusted that kid—but he didn't.

Before he got his gear together, Jesse went to find Molly.

"So, were the berries good out there, Molly?"

Her eyes narrowed in suspicion. "I dropped my basket of berries when I saw the bears. What's it to you?"

"There were no berry bushes there," he said.

"I ran to that area to get away from the bears. The berries were in another place."

He studied her for a beat. "Do you have a cell phone, Molly?"

"Of course. What of it?"

"Is there reception out in that end of the valley?"

"I wouldn't know—I didn't try to call anyone."

"Not even for help when you saw the bears?"

"Who would I call—Samuel? Yeah, right, wiseass. And I couldn't call anyone in the house, because, *duh,* no reception."

With one hundred bucks in his pocket, cowboy hat tilted low over his brow and a backpack on his shoulder, Jesse threw June a broad grin. It made his blue eyes twinkle against his tan, and it made June's stomach heat.

"You look like you're actually champing at the bit to get out into those mountains with my dog."

"I am," he said. "I'm going to find myself. Maybe the search dog at my side will help."

In spite of his upbeat mood, June felt anxious. She hoped the answers he did find were the ones he wanted. Crouching down, she hugged Eager, burying her face in his fur for a moment. And the idea of possibly losing her dog with a stranger suddenly filled her eyes with emotion.

"I won't lose him," he said.

"You managed to lose yourself, big guy—I'm not sure I can take your word for it." She ruffled Eager's fur. "Look after the cowboy, Eager." She got to her feet, pushed a fall of hair back from her face and her gaze met Jesse's.

"Take care. And don't forget to give Eager water."

Jesse leaned forward suddenly, grasped her wrist and pulled her toward him. Tilting her chin up, he kissed her softly on the mouth.

June's world spiraled as her lips opened under his. She kissed him back, suddenly hungry, desperate, her tongue seeking his, her hands going up his muscled arms, hooking behind his neck, drawing him down, kissing him deeper.

He pulled away suddenly, a strange and dangerous look in his eyes, the pulse at his neck throbbing.

"Be careful, June." His voice was thick, hoarse.

June stepped back, aching inside for something she wasn't sure she could have.

"See you at Dixon's," she said.

He nodded.

She hesitated a moment, then with a quick glance at Eager, she swung her own pack onto her back and headed toward the boardwalk that led to the tunnel entrance. She didn't look back. But she knew he was watching.

Even when she reached the tunnel, she wouldn't look back. She told herself it was a dangerous game, to fall for a perfect stranger, a man who had another, as yet, secret life. She was going to get burned. And June couldn't afford to get burned by a relationship again.

June hiked along the ridge where Davis said he'd found the baby's pacifier. This route would bring her down to Hannah's farm via a trail on the eastern flank. The day was clear and hot, the sun bright. She could see Cold Plains in the valley below; such a pretty storybook town on the surface, such dark secrets it harbored.

She shaded her eyes and glanced up at the steep slope of giant black boulders on her left. It was almost as sheer as a cliff, and she knew it to be riddled with small caves—this whole area was pocked with caves. She'd helped search this boulder slope when Rafe's baby had been taken, and it had come up clean. But given the pacifier that Davis had found here, June wondered if the kidnapper might have backtracked and be holed up with the baby somewhere in there now. A sinister chill unfurled inside her, and an eerie sense of being watched prickled over her skin. With it came a whisper of fear. She didn't want to go up there and face a kidnapper alone. She'd return with Jesse and Eager. June marked the location on her GPS, and as she continued along the trail she realized she was thinking of Jesse as an ally, and it felt damn good to have one.

Be careful, June.

By the time she reached the ribbon of paved road that led to Hannah's ranch, the August sun was high and burning down hot on her head. A black SUV approached from the distance. As it neared, it slowed.

It was Mayor Kittridge. He pulled off onto the shoulder and rolled down the window, sticking his elbow out.

June cursed under her breath.

"Mr. Mayor!" she said with an exaggerated smile as she came up to the side of his vehicle.

"Hello, June." He looked tired, most likely from his nighttime search for Jesse. She spied a rifle on the backseat. Caution skittered through her.

He was eyeing her pack. "Where've you been? Where's Eager today?"

Thank God she'd taken the effort to come down via the eastern flank. "Eager's at the vet," she said. "He was bitten by something. I'm going to get him this afternoon." And before he could press for specifics, she glanced at her watch.

"I must be off to fetch him now. I'd like to be back in time for the corn roast. Hopefully Hannah and her new help will join me."

Interest, sharp and sudden, crossed Kittridge's features.

He tried to hide it with his easy smile, but his eyes lied. A newcomer in Cold Plains was going to be of interest to the mayor, especially so if said mayor was also one of Samuel's militia leaders.

June still couldn't see anything in Rufus Kittridge's face that would indicate he was a coldhearted killer. How did one ever know they were looking into the eyes of a murderer? This place was so damned creepy, it made her sick.

"What help?" said Kittridge.

"She's hiring an old friend of mine—old boyfriend, actually—for some heavy-duty lifting on the ranch. Hannah's feeling her age and I think it's a good thing she's finally admitting she needs more help. My friend is flying into Little Gulch. I'm going to pick him up when I go get Eager."

Anxious he'd ask for specifics, and that he and Chief Fargo might team up and go investigating in Little Gulch, June quickly changed the subject.

"Will you be there?"

"Where?" he said, suddenly distracted.

"At the corn roast."

"Of course. I—"

"Well, see you there." She turned to go. "I must leave to fetch Eager or I won't make it back in time," she called cheerily, giving a jaunty wave. Her heart hammered in her chest.

He drove off, slowly.

June's mouth was dry as she crossed the field to the outbuilding she rented from Hannah. She moved quickly. Hannah needed to be apprised of the details of the plan June had cooked up before anyone else spoke to her.

When June drove out of town twenty minutes later, she glanced uneasily into the rearview mirror. It was one thing to be seen driving out of town without her dog, quite another to be followed. To her relief the road was empty as she left Cold Plains.

She put her foot on the gas, wound down the window, and the wind blew warm through her hair as the fields of rural southeastern Wyoming rolled by. Gradually, as she clocked the miles between herself and Cold Plains, she began to relax, and June realized suddenly what a deep and negative toll the perfectly evil town and its Devotees were taking on her. Jesse's words crept into her mind.

You can't keep this up, June. You've got to find a way to slow down.

Jesse was at Dixon's Pub, sitting at a wooden picnic table in the shade of a trellis in the beer garden out back. Eager snoozed at his feet, a water bowl near his head. June's heart clutched at the sight of them—man and dog, good and tired from their trek over the mountain.

Eager sensed her presence instantly, lifting his head then surging to his feet, body wiggling as he came toward her. June felt surprise at her sudden surge of emotions again. Everything was riding just a little too close to the surface. She had to tamp this down.

She dropped down to her haunches and ruffled her dog's coat. "Good boy, Eager. You made it. You showed him how to get over the mountains, did you?"

She avoided looking up, but she had to eventually. Jesse had gotten to his feet and was standing near the table, giving her space. He smiled, teeth bright white, stubble shadowing his strong jaw.

His tan had deepened during the hours of hiking. He'd shucked the denim shirt and his white T-shirt was taut over his pecs. His jeans were dusty. His jacket hung over the bench next to the pack she'd loaned him, but he'd kept his hat on.

Damn, he looked good. She thought of their last kiss and

a nervousness, excitement, raced quietly through her blood. For a moment she wished he could be just Jesse. No hidden past. And that she could be just June.

She got to her feet, brushing back strands of hair from her face.

"You made it," she said.

"So did you. It's good to see you." His grin deepened. "I got to thinking, as long as I have your dog you're not going to abandon me."

Something sobered inside June, and she knew by those words he was feeling vulnerable, too.

"Can I get you a beer?" he said.

"A cold one would be excellent." The August afternoon was sweltering. Country music floated softy through the open doors into the beer garden. No one else was sitting outside. A few hard-time drinkers and ranch hands lingered inside, playing pool, minding their drinks.

Jesse motioned to a young server who brought two ice-cold beers, the bottles sweating with condensation.

"It's on me," June said, reaching for her wallet in her back pocket.

He placed his hand on her arm. "No."

"Jesse," she whispered, "that's all the money you have to your name right now. You might need it."

"I still think I have a big bank account that I can't remember."

"Yeah, dream on, buddy."

He paid the server and June took a deep swig right from the bottle, relishing the soft, cold explosion of bubbles in her mouth, the scent of hay being cut a distance away, the warmth of the afternoon. And, slowly, a decompressing sensation filled her body.

"I haven't done anything like this in ages." She stretched

her legs out and scratched Eager's neck with the toe of her boot.

"When we get back to the cave house," Jesse said over his bottle, "after we're through with the dog-and-pony show at the corn roast, what can I help you guys with?"

She liked his positivity. It bolstered her.

"Hannah hasn't got anyone who needs to be evacuated right now. But I could do with your help on another front." She hesitated, taking another swig of her beer, deciding how best to tell the story.

"There's a doctor in town, Rafe Black, whose baby boy was kidnapped last month. Rafe is not a Devotee, but some time ago he had a relationship with one of the five victims believed to have been murdered by Samuel or his men. Her name was Abby Michaels. She had a baby boy and when the child was three months old, she contacted Rafe and told him the boy was his. Rafe believed her. He sent her money and then came to town to find her. But Abby and the alleged infant had disappeared."

"Alleged?"

June nodded. "No one in Cold Plains would attest to Abby actually having a baby, but she'd sent Rafe a photo, and he believed her. Then, two months ago a baby boy—a dead ringer for the photo Abby had sent Rafe—was left on Bo Fargo's desk at the police detachment. He was strapped into a car seat with a note pinned to him saying he was Devin Black. Rafe was overjoyed."

"Jesus, that's weird. Where'd the kid suddenly appear from?"

"No one knows. The note was anonymous. The person who wrote it said they'd found Devin abandoned, and they'd taken him and fallen in love with him. But when they heard Dr. Black was looking for his son, they felt duty-bound to give him back."

Jesse sipped his beer. "How did this anonymous person get all the way into a police detachment and leave a child in a car seat on the chief's desk without being seen?"

"Again, no one seems to know, or if they do, they're not saying. Rafe was nevertheless thrilled to have found his son. Then last month, while Devin was sleeping in Rafe's house, he was taken."

Jesse whistled. "It must've killed the doc."

"He's distraught. There's been no ransom note, and the police have no leads. Teams searched the mountains, but Bo Fargo called off the search pretty quickly, as if he didn't actually want this kidnapper found."

"What about the feds?"

"They've got no leads, either."

"So how do you need my help?"

June checked her watch. It was getting late—they needed to leave if they wanted to be back for the corn roast. "Last night when Davis was tracking the henchmen he found a baby's pacifier under a slope riddled with caves. The caves were searched after the kidnapping, but I think there's a chance the kidnapper could have returned and holed up in one of those caves. I'd like to take Eager up there, but I didn't want to go alone."

"So you want me to come?"

"You can be my armed backup." She smiled.

But his eyes narrowed. "This is for the police, June."

"Are you kidding me? Bo Fargo *is* the police in Cold Plains, and Fargo is Samuel's puppet. If Samuel doesn't want that kidnapper found, Fargo's not going to find him."

"Is that what you think happened?"

"I don't know—like you said, it's weird how a baby in a car seat can suddenly appear on the police chief's desk with no one seeing a thing. And then the search was called off prematurely. I haven't seen Fargo or his men doing a thing more to investigate the case since then."

"The FBI should be on it."

"You're right. But the agents Hawk Bledsoe brought with him to Cold Plains are suits, not SAR technicians. They'd still need to bring in dogs, trained searchers. By the time they get those kinds of resources together the kidnapper could be long gone. His scent trail will be cold. Eager is right here. He could track from the location the pacifier was found. If we come across something, we notify the feds."

Jesse was silent for several beats. "We'll talk about it, okay? But we should probably head out now."

June sighed heavily.

He placed his hand over hers. "Hey, I just don't want you to get hurt."

He fingered her wedding band.

June swallowed, feeling suddenly uncomfortable.

"Matt was a lucky man, you know that?"

"If he was lucky, I would have saved him."

"June?"

She looked up into his indigo eyes.

"You can't keep carrying guilt."

"What of it? I'm doing good work because of what happened."

"It'll crush you eventually. You're afraid to let it go, aren't you? You're scared you'll have nothing left then."

Irritation flared in her. "I don't need a shrink, Jesse. Maybe you should sort out your own demons before you cast stones." June got up abruptly, but he grasped her arm.

"June, I care for you."

"Please, don't touch me. I—I can't do this. It's not going to work. I have no idea who you are. You might have a family or something waiting for you."

I couldn't bear to lose someone again.

"Fine," he said, letting her go. "Let's go get this over with." His voice was brusque, and his movements were angry as he led her and Eager out through the dim pub interior and into the parking lot at the front of the establishment.

Big trucks and a Harley were parked outside. Heat waves oscillated off the paving. Above the building the *D* in the pink neon sign that read Dixon's Pub and Beer Garden flickered like a Devotee omen.

June felt a swish of nerves return as she climbed into her truck cab. She fired the ignition, and, as she pulled out of the lot, Eager sitting between her and a heavily silent Jesse, she told herself it was going to be fine. He'd find out who he was, go home. And Hawk would get something on Samuel, arrest him, and then she could go on to a new job in another state.

The late-evening sun lingered gold over the picture-perfect town as June drove into Cold Plains. Smoke curled from the barbecues on the lawn outside the community centre and crowds gathered around the food tents. A band played on a stand at the far end where tiny colored lights had been strung up. Already, some of the townsfolk were dancing.

Laughing kids gamboled on the grass, and mothers with smiling faces pushed strollers, husbands at their sides, offering greetings to neighbors as they passed. A bitter taste filled June's mouth.

She glanced at Jesse, felt his tension

"Remember, it's all in the attitude," he said as he tilted his cowboy hat a tad lower over his eyes. "If you believe the story, so will they."

She nodded, slowed and waved at Chief Bo Fargo, who was over by the main tent, talking to Mayor Kittridge. Both turned to look. Fargo began to walk over the lawn toward the truck.

"Oh, Jesus," she whispered. "Party time."

She stopped the truck, wound down the window. Eager gave a soft growl. He didn't like Fargo any more than she did. The man had a bad vibe, even for dogs.

"Hey, Bo," June said cheerily. "I just wanted to say thanks for letting me off the SAR hook the other day. I really needed that seminar. It's always good to hear Samuel speak. Gives one a real boost."

Fargo's watery blue gaze darted over her truck, then he peered into the cab, his attention on Jesse.

"So Eager's better?" he said.

"One hundred percent. I just went to fetch him. In fact, I got two for one." June forced a grin. "This here is Jesse... Marlboro. He's an old friend of mine from back West. Hannah needed some help on the ranch and—" she shot Jesse a look "—I volunteered him." She forced a big smile.

Jesse placed his hand on her knee and June tensed inside. But it was a good call, because Fargo noted the gesture.

Behind him Mayor Rufus Kittridge was hurrying over the grass toward them now.

"Well, we should find some parking." As she spoke, June could see Samuel watching them from under another tent. Her chest tightened.

It's all in the attitude.

Kittridge was coming closer.

"You guys going to stay for the dance?" Fargo addressed Jesse.

"You betcha," Jesse said with an easy grin.

June pulled off, found parking and turned off the ignition. She sat silent awhile, gathering herself, her heart hammering.

Jesse said, "Marlboro?"

"Just came to me." Then she snapped, "We should have worked this out in more detail. We should have had a surname ready." She turned in the seat to face him. "So, does being here jog your memory—do you recall *anything?*"

"Not a damn thing," he said. "I've never been to this place in my life. I'm sure of it. Nothing at all feels familiar about it."

"But you came here sporting a *D* tattoo," she said, exasperation creeping into her voice. "You *knew* about this place, about Samuel."

"Let's go eat and dance, June," he said quietly. "Then tomorrow morning we go to the caves, early."

She inhaled deeply, staring at him. Then nodded. "Thank you."

"Samuel, that was an excellent seminar," June said, putting her cob of corn down onto her paper plate as Samuel Grayson approached her and Jesse's table. They were eating under the colored lights that had been strung up near the dancing area where the band cranked out a feisty country tune.

Samuel's eyes, however, were fixed solely on Jesse, and June knew he *had* to be wondering if Jesse was the mystery man from the woods.

Jesse got to his feet and warmly held out his hand. "Jesse Marlboro—pleased to finally meet you. I've heard so much about you from June."

Samuel shook Jesse's hand firmly and smiled. "Samuel Grayson."

"This is a great event," Jesse said, hooking his thumbs into his belt. Inwardly June smiled.

"It's a celebration of being the best town we can be," Samuel said. "And it's a nod to the approaching end of summer, hence the berry desserts, the corn on the cob, the burgers."

"Please, take a seat." Jesse gestured to the table, his demeanor assertive, confident, but warm. June was amazed.

He was totally engaging, friendly, yet always alpha, and so very far removed from an image of an injured man in the dark woods that she began to believe he was actually going to pull this off.

"Don't mind if I do, but just for a few," Samuel said, swinging his leg over the picnic bench and seating himself. He gave his trademark Pierce Brosnan–style smile, his twinkling green sociopath's eyes belying whatever was going on in his mind.

"June has been telling me about your seminars and explaining the philosophy behind Cold Plains, and when I hit a rough patch workwise, and she mentioned Hannah was looking for a hand on the ranch, I thought it would be perfect to try and start fresh." He threw June a glance then smiled conspiratorially at Samuel. "And then there's June."

She felt her cheeks flush in spite of the situation.

"Mayor Kittridge tells me that you two used to date."

So he'd already spread the word about the stranger's imminent arrival.

"Off and on," she said. "Before Jesse found work on the rig."

"Oh, really, which rig?"

"Off the coast of Nigeria," Jesse said quickly. "I know, it was far, foreign, but I—I needed cash." He snorted. "And there were no casinos out there. I thought I'd be able to square some savings away." He placed his hand over June's. "Then the job fizzled—labor unrest, political upheaval. Nigeria is not an easy place to do business. I went on a bit of a downer." He inhaled, squaring his shoulders. "But hey, now I'm here. *And* there are no casinos."

Samuel was watching him closely. Then he smiled, cautiously, thought June, like a shark.

"Sounds like you'll be a very good match for our community, Jesse." He stood up, holding out his hand again. "And a good match for June. Pleased to have met you, Jesse. Hope to see you at my next seminar."

"You betcha."

They sat in silence watching Samuel stride over to the next table, doing his rounds.

The band had switched to a slow, sad tune. Couples were swaying quietly to the music, holding each other close. The air was warm.

"Christ," muttered Jesse. "That's the second time I've used 'you betcha' tonight." He repositioned his hat, scrubbed his brow. "Like some cowpoke."

"Nigeria?" she asked.

Then they both laughed.

"Hey," June said, giving him a mock punch, "I think you pulled that off great."

"And you look beautiful tonight, you know that?"

"Jesse," she warned.

"Just stating a fact. Come, dance with me."

"I don't think that's a good idea. I—"

He got up, took her hand. "Samuel's watching," he murmured. "It's a *very* good idea."

Swaying to the music with June in his arms couldn't have felt more right to Jesse. Her curves fitted perfectly against his body, and her hair smelled of lavender. He liked the way it felt against his cheeks. He enjoyed the sensation of her breasts pressing firmly against his torso, the way she moved against him.

He glanced down and saw that her eyes were closed. Heat speared to his groin.

"Would be nice to have a beer," he murmured against her hair.

"I'm afraid you're looking at a choice between a $25 bottle

of water. Or a $25 bottle of water. There's no overt consumption of alcohol in Cold Plains."

"So the food at the festival is free, but the water is not?"

"It never is, even though it comes straight from a creek. Samuel's people bottle it for him without being paid. He sells it back to them and pockets one hundred percent of the profits."

"You're kidding me?"

"'Fraid not."

Jesse whistled softly. "It's like a freaking Stepford town. Reminds me of that movie *The Truman Show*. You feel like someone is watching you from a control tower."

"You *are* being watched," she said quietly, nestling against his arm as she moved. Jesse stirred, his jeans going tight.

"Samuel is the control tower. That was good, by the way, what you said about hitting a rough patch and the gambling. He's going to home right in on it, perceive it as your weakness."

The music changed, another slow tune.

June pulled back. She looked tired.

"I think we can make an exit now," she said. "We still need to drive back to Hannah's ranch and then hike in to the cave house."

Eager, who'd been sleeping in the truck, thumped his tail with excitement to see them. But as June was about to climb up into the driver's seat, Jesse placed his hand on her arm.

"Let me drive," he said. "You look beat."

She hesitated, then handed him her keys. "Gee, thanks."

"Beat but still beautiful."

"Flattery will get you everywhere," she said as she climbed into the passenger seat. She didn't want to admit it to herself, but she was beyond exhaustion now. She gave him directions to Hannah's ranch, and as they drove, she felt herself nodding in and out of sleep.

"He's powerful, got big charisma," Jesse said as he wheeled the truck onto the dirt road that led to Hannah's house. "I can see why Samuel has pull over people."

"But seeing Samuel doesn't bring anything back? You still have no idea why you wanted to come here, why his name was familiar to you?"

"Nothing," he said. "Not a goddamn thing. I don't know any of those people from a bar of soap."

"Maybe it'll come still."

"Yeah, maybe."

About half an hour after introducing Hannah to Jesse, he and June were hiking up the trail into the mountains again, small headlamps lighting their way through the darkness. Before they headed out of cell-tower range, June once again tried to contact Agent Hawk Bledsoe but the call went straight to voice mail, which said he'd be back day after tomorrow.

The cave tunnel was dark, spooky. Jesse had only vague recollections of coming through here with June the first time. She was brave, he decided as he felt a bat flutter past his face. Braver than any woman he'd known.

He stilled in the darkness. How many women had he known?

Another image came to him. Making love to a slight, dark-haired woman with fiery blue eyes; a raw, shocking sadness ripped through him. Then there was nothing, just a feeling of depression and the now sickly familiar chill of guilt. Jesse was relieved to finally exit the tunnel, but the cold, dark sense of guilt lingered with him.

He paused outside the door of the cave house. June was right. He couldn't do this to her, to himself—or to whoever might be waiting somewhere in this world for him to come home. He had to know who that dark-haired woman was before he could even think of touching June again.

"You can take one of the spare rooms," June said as they entered the hallway.

He nodded as she closed and locked the front door behind him.

He watched while she went to her own room and he heard the door snick shut. A hollowness filled his heart.

Chapter 8

By the time June, Jesse and Eager reached the base of the boulder slope, the morning sun was hot, the east-facing black rocks absorbing heat and radiating it back at them like an oven.

Eager was panting hard, his black coat soaking up heat, too. June stopped to give him water while Jesse scanned the horizon, hand shading his eyes. From this vantage point he could see for miles.

He carried a loaded shotgun in his hand and his Beretta in the holster at his hip—June had returned it to him. She carried her own weapon.

Once Eager was watered, June panned the rock wall above them with her binoculars, considering search strategy.

"We need to get up to that ridge on top of the boulder face," she said, pointing.

"Why?"

"The heat rising from these rocks is causing upward air currents. If there is human scent in the caves, it will rise with the currents to that ridge. I need to work Eager across the currents. If he picks something up, he can zero down onto the scent cone."

Tension rippled softly through Jesse as he squinted up at the boulder face. He tried to imagine a kidnapper with a baby up there in one of the dark holes, and he wondered how long an infant could possibly survive. An image sliced through his brain again—a baby screaming, and the dark-haired woman yelling for help. The same woman he'd slept with.

Flames crackled suddenly through his mind, devouring the image, and he felt searing heat. Jesse shook himself. The heat was from the rocks, the sun. But it unsettled him. He *had* to find out what those haunting images meant, or he would not be able to go forward. Seemed he couldn't go back, either. He was trapped in a web of present.

"Okay," he said quietly. "We go up, but we go around that way." He pointed to a talus slope to the left of the giant boulder wall.

"The ground inclines less sharply over there, and we won't be visible to anyone who might be hiding in one of the caves above. You go first," he said, eyeing caves, unable to shake an eerie sensation of being watched. "I've got your back." He clicked the safety off the shotgun.

June began to clamber up the shale slope, small stones skittering out from under her boots. Eager bounded easily ahead of her, unleashing his own shower of tiny rocks. Jesse waited until there was a bit of distance between June and the small avalanche of shale she and her dog were creating.

And as he waited, he watched June climb.

Her red hair hung in a neat braid down the middle of her back. She was wearing a lightweight khaki shirt, rugged cargo pants and hiking boots with gaiters. Her SAR pack, he knew, contained a first-aid kit, water and other survival essentials. She carried her radio in a vest pouch at her front for easy access.

The sun made her hair shine and exertion made her skin gleam, and she climbed with athletic grace. He suddenly wondered what she was like in bed. The idea made him hard.

Abruptly, she raised her hand, pointed. With her other hand she was restraining Eager by his harness. The dog's tail was wagging and his vision was totally focused on something he'd detected in the rocks to their right.

Jesse scrambled quickly up the shale behind her.

"What is it?" he whispered when he reached her side.

"Eager scented something," she said very quietly as she pointed. "It has to be something in that cave over there."

"Good boy," she whispered, hooking a leash into Eager's harness. "Leave it for now.

"I don't want to let him go," she explained to Jesse. "It could be dangerous for him if the kidnapper is holed up in there."

"There's no way for us to approach at all without being seen," he said softly.

They watched quietly, in silence, trying to detect movement. The sun bore down on them. Jesse could hear the soft sound of bees somewhere, the sharp cry of a bird up high, Eager's panting.

June's gaze went to the bird of prey circling high above them. There was a second bird wheeling on air currents even higher.

"Not a good sign," she whispered. "Those birds are often the first indication a search has turned into a recovery mission. Once when—" She froze suddenly and then gripped Jesse's arm.

"Did you hear that?" she whispered

Jesse angled his head. "What?"

Then suddenly he caught the sound—a mewl. His heart slammed into his rib cage. *Baby!*

Crying.

Oh, Jesus. He lunged blindly forward, images slamming into him. He could hear the fire coming. Crackling. Roaring. The baby's screams growing louder and louder and louder in his head. His baby. Going to die! Got to save him!

Jesse scrambled wildly across the boulders toward the cave, toward the sound, toward his son. Perspiration drenched his shirt, trickled down his brow. Small stones clattered loudly down the slope.

"Jesse!" June hissed. "Stop! What…in hell are you doing!"

She began to clamber after him, panic lacing through her. It was as though some switch had triggered in him, and he'd gone stark, raving mad. She reached him as he struggled to ascend a large slab of rock to the cave above, and she grabbed his ankle.

"Jesse!' Her heart was racing.

He spun around, eyes wild. He was wire-tense, muscles amped, sweat soaking his T-shirt, gleaming on his face. He looked totally unfocused, dazed.

"What's going on, Jesse? *Talk* to me."

His hand went to his brow. His eyes seemed to come back into focus. Then shock rippled through his features as he re-alized what he'd just done.

"Come down here," she said softly. "Come under this over-hang before someone tries to fire on us or throw rocks from above."

He allowed himself to slide down and he slumped back against the rock under the slab he'd been trying to mount. He was breathing hard.

"What happened, Jesse?" she whispered, gathering Eager to her side, thinking they might have put themselves in a real bad spot. If they tried to move now, they'd be sitting ducks.

At the same time, June could still hear the baby crying above them somewhere. Tension coiled through her stomach.

Rafe's son?

And someone had to be with the infant—it could not have survived up here by itself. A mix of urgency, thrill, fear, cocktailed through her.

"I thought I was…in another time, another place," Jesse was saying. He raked his hand through his hair, which was damp with perspiration.

June offered him water, and he drank deeply. Head injuries were strange things, she thought as she watched him. Perhaps she should take him to the hospital in Little Gulch.

"I thought it was another baby," he said finally, his voice hoarse.

"Whose baby, Jesse?"

His features twisted with some inner anguish. "I…" His gaze met her eyes square, held for a moment.

"I don't know."

She held his gaze, wondering if it was a lie. And something slipped inside her chest.

"I thought there was fire."

"What happened in the fire?"

He shook his head, pain in his eyes. "I don't know."

"Jesse—" But she stilled at the sound of a male voice coming from above them.

"Hello! Who's there?"

They both froze.

"Can anyone hear me?"

"Go that way, Jesse," she whispered, pointing to the far side of the overhang. "I'll create a distraction by stepping out from under the overhang on the opposite side. You keep me covered from the rocks on the far side."

He inhaled, collecting himself, and nodded.

"Eager, you park here. Park, boy." Her dog sat, his body tense as he watched her intently with his trusting brown eyes.

June tossed a rock out from under the overhang. It clattered loudly, starting a diversion. Jesse began to move.

She called out loudly, "I'm coming out. I'm unarmed."

June stepped out from under the rock overhang. Out of the corner of her eye she saw Jesse with his gun ready. He nodded.

June edged out into full view, hands to her side, palms open.

A man stood on a rock slab above her, tousled dark hair blowing in the hot breeze. He was slender, young. Pale face. No weapon in his hands.

His T-shirt was stained with dirt.

"My name is June Farrow," she called up to him. In her peripheral vision, June saw Jesse creeping higher up the side of the ridge. He placed shotgun stock to shoulder, drawing a bead on the young man.

"I thought I heard a baby crying," she called.

"Where's the guy you were with? I saw two of you coming up."

"He's still under the ledge below me," June lied. "He twisted his ankle when he tried to climb too fast. He's resting it."

"I know you," the young man said. "You're from Cold Plains. You're the K9 search-and-rescue handler. I recognize your red hair and the dog. Where's the dog now?"

"With my friend."

She racked her brain. He was vaguely familiar, but she couldn't place him.

"What's your name?"

"Tyler."

"Tyler who?"

He hesitated, and June saw him glancing over his shoulder. A small hatchet of panic struck her chest.

"Did you take Dr. Black's baby, Tyler? Is that who we can hear crying?"

"No," he said. "I took my baby."

Go easy, June—he could be delusional, thinking Rafe's child is his.

"Do you know where Dr. Black's baby is, Tyler?"

"It *wasn't* his baby!" She saw he was shaking. And she thought she could see the glimmer of tears running down his face. "It never *was* his baby! Samuel Grayson's men made me leave my own son at the police station so Chief Fargo could pretend it was Dr. Black's boy."

Jesus.

"Okay, Tyler, listen to me. I'm coming up."

"No! You're *not* going to take my baby."

"I'm not going to take your son, Tyler." June climbed up as she called out to the young man. "I want to help you both. I have a first-aid kit in my pack. I have water, food. Are you hungry, Tyler?"

He nodded. As she got closer, June deduced Tyler was maybe in his early twenties—a very young father, if he was telling the truth.

Where was the mother?

June reached the slab of rock that jutted out in front of the cave and climbed up. Tyler shot a nervous glance into the dark space behind him.

"Is the baby in there, Tyler? Do you mind if I call my friend and dog up? They can help."

Uncertainty crossed his face. His eyes were huge with fear, his skin bloodless. His shirt hung loose over a gaunt frame. He'd been trying to live in the wilderness for some time, thought June. She hoped the baby was okay.

June signaled to Jesse and whistled for Eager, then she

ducked quickly into the darkness of the cave. It was hot inside, the air still.

The baby was lying on a wad of clothing. Silent now.

Too silent. Her heart dropped

"He's fine," Tyler said. "We just ran out of formula this morning. I go into town after dark and steal it from the day care—there's a window that doesn't lock."

The infant indeed had a good pulse. It wasn't emaciated. And it was sleeping now, having cried itself out. June shot Tyler a glance.

"Do you leave the baby here when you go thieving?" She shrugged out of her pack as she spoke.

He hesitated. "I—I don't know what else to do."

June cursed under her breath. "You're lucky as the blazes. There are wild animals in these mountains. You—" June stopped. Tears were rolling down the young man's face and he was shaking hard.

She examined the infant in silence. There were no bruises, cuts. Its little limbs seemed fine. Emotion, relief burned into her own eyes as her adrenaline began to ebb.

She gathered the baby boy into her arms and sat with him out in the sun on the plateau, just holding him for a while, Tyler watching.

Jesse had come up onto the ledge with Eager. He stared at the baby boy, his features tightening. He shot a fierce look at Tyler.

"I was scared," Tyler said softly.

"What's the baby's name, Tyler?" June said.

"Aiden."

She felt blood drain from her head. Speech eluded her for several moments. When she spoke, her voice came out hoarse. "It's a good name."

Jesse was watching her intently now. She knew he understood the significance—it was the name of her own dead son.

"Where's Aiden's mother?" June asked, her voice thick.

"She's dead." Tyler suddenly sank down onto the rock and clutched his arms around his knees, rocking slightly.

Compassion mushroomed in June's chest, along with a cool whisper of suspicion.

"Tyler," she said, "I'm going to ask you a question, and you need to trust me with the answer. You need to be honest. Are you a Devotee?"

Fear, almost sheer terror, whitened his face.

"I can help you if you are, Tyler. You won't ever have to go back to Cold Plains."

"No police?"

"Not the Cold Plains police."

"I'm not a Devotee, but my wife was."

"Aiden's mother?"

He nodded.

"Tell us about her. Tell us what happened with Chief Fargo, and why you left Aiden on his desk."

He began to rock again.

"Aiden's mother's name was Sally. We got married against Samuel's will. We did it in Cheyenne. But we came back— we should never have come back."

"Why did you?"

Tyler sniffed, rubbed his nose. "Work. I'm a mechanic, and I could get work in Cold Plains. We needed money. Sally still believed in Samuel. She was confused. He promised her things she didn't have, that I couldn't give. Samuel had wanted her to marry an older guy. He was furious when he learned she'd married me instead and was carrying my baby. But even though he was mad as hell, Samuel still wanted to do private counseling sessions with Sally. I—I don't know why she listened to him, why she went." Emotion surged and his voice cracked.

June's heart cracked. She thought of Matt, of how illogical his behavior had seemed to her toward the end.

"He took her for several counseling sessions after she had the baby, then when she told Samuel she was going to move back to Cheyenne with me, she had the accident."

"What kind of accident?" Jesse interjected.

Tyler glanced nervously at him, then June. "She drowned in the lake. I think he killed her. I'm *convinced* he killed her. I—I think he was sleeping with her, too." Tears sheened down his cheeks.

Rage arrowed through June's heart. If Tyler was telling the truth, it could make Sally murder victim number six. And June believed more of Samuel's victims would yet surface.

"I asked for an investigation," Tyler said. "But Chief Fargo claimed it was obvious that her death was an accident. I *know* it wasn't. Sally never went near the lake. She couldn't swim. She was afraid of water."

"And you've been caring for Aiden since she died?"

He nodded. Tears welling again. "One of the people from the Urgent Care Center came to take him away. They said they looked after babies like Aiden. But I refused to let him go. I began to make secret plans to leave, and I started saving money. But then a guy called Jason Barnes and his friend Lumpy Smithers came to talk to me. I knew they were henchmen. They said I must leave Aiden with Bo Fargo and write a note saying my son was Devin Black."

June's throat went dry.

"They said they were going to give Aiden to Dr. Black to keep the community whole. I was given two days to make up my mind. Then, when I went to work the next morning, I discovered I'd been fired. I came home and my landlord said I owed him two months rent, which was a lie. He gave me notice at the same time. My truck was stolen, and my bank account was frozen." He swallowed. "Then Jason Barnes returned and said maybe I better do as he asked—they had contacts, and things would get worse for me if I didn't obey them."

"Did Jason say Samuel sent him?" Jesse said.

"No, but I know Jason Barnes works for Samuel."

So, no evidence to pin on Samuel himself, thought June. That bastard was like Teflon.

"I had no place to stay. No money, no work, no transport. I was afraid for my life, and they promised Aiden would be well cared for by Dr. Black. So I did as they said. Then…I— I just couldn't handle it. I kidnapped my own son back, and we had nowhere to go so we hid in the mountains."

"You have a safe place now, Tyler. We're going to take you and Aiden there. This is my friend Jesse. He—" she met his eyes "—helps me. And this is Eager." She smiled. "Eager helps just about anyone who lets him. If he doesn't first love them to death."

Tyler gave a tremulous smile and tears pooled again in his eyes. "Thank you, June," he whispered.

"Hey, it's what I do. And you know what, Tyler?" She glanced down at the baby sleeping in her arms. "It's worth every moment."

She felt Jesse's large hand on her shoulder. He squeezed. And June had to struggle to tamp down her own emotions.

Later that day, back in the safe house, Jesse sat near the hearth feeding Aiden from a baby bottle. Tyler was sleeping and June was busy in the kitchen making sandwiches. He could feel her watching him, though, and when he glanced up and met her gaze, there was a strange look on her face.

"What is it?" he said.

She inhaled deeply, turned away.

"You're thinking about your Aiden, aren't you?"

She stilled, her nose going slightly pink and her eyes

watery. "I was thinking how good you look holding that baby," she said quietly. She picked up a knife and dug it into a pot of mayo. "You look experienced," she said.

There was an odd tone in her voice, almost accusatory.

She spread the mayonnaise over a slice of bread, her movements jerky, a little angry.

"Back at the cave, when you thought it was another baby crying, when you thought there was a fire—are you *sure* you don't remember whose baby was in your mind?"

So that was it, thought Jesse. She hadn't believed him when he'd told her he didn't know.

He glanced down at the dark-haired infant in his arms. The baby in his memory was dark-haired, too. And he'd believed in that blinding instant that it *had* been his child. But on the back of that feeling rode another, harder sensation, one that told him while the baby in his memory *was* somehow connected to him, it also wasn't. It was the same mixed-up conflict he had over the hazy memory of the slight, dark-haired woman—the woman he remembered making love to at some point; the woman who brought on emotions of guilt, rage, hurt, sorrow. The woman who made him finger an absent ring.

"I don't know what baby I saw," he said quietly, and Jesse didn't feel he was lying to June. He couldn't honestly say one way or the other whose baby he was remembering, and he also didn't want to express his doubts about it to June because he didn't want to chase her away.

"I need to go tell Rafe Black about Tyler and his son. Rafe's going to be devastated." She bagged the sandwiches and reached into the fridge for a bottle of water. She put it all into her pack.

"*We* need to go tell Rafe," he said, getting up, the baby still in his arms.

June braced both hands on the counter and dropped her

head. She was silent for several beats. Then she looked up, a strange determination in her eyes. "I need to go alone, Jesse."

"June—"

She spun around and marched out of the kitchen, leaving her pack on the counter.

Jesse quickly went to find Lacy and he handed baby Aiden into her care.

When he came back into the living area, June was near the front door lacing up her hiking boots. Her face had been washed and her eyes were red-rimmed. Her mouth was set in a tight line.

"So you believe Tyler's story, June?" he said.

"Yeah, I do. Rafe will want a DNA test for proof, of course, but I believe the baby is Tyler's."

"Do you think Rafe's baby even exists?"

"He believes his son is out there somewhere." She got up, swung her pack onto her shoulders.

"We had a deal, June."

She stilled, hand on the door. "What deal was that?"

"I help you—you help me. We work as a team. I'm coming with you."

"It hurts to be with you, Jesse."

"Why?"

"You know why," she said quietly. "And I think you're lying to me. I think you have a baby, and that means a woman in your life."

"It *doesn't* mean a woman in my life. And, June, I'm not lying. I won't do anything to hurt you. I promise you that."

"How can you promise me anything?" she said crisply. "You don't even know who you are."

She stomped out of the house.

Jesse grabbed his gear and followed. The fact she didn't try to stop him gave Jesse a small flare of hope.

* * *

It was late afternoon by the time Jesse and June were sitting with Dr. Rafe Black at his kitchen table watching his fiancée, Darcy, making coffee. The doctor was a dark-haired man with serious brown eyes and a kind demeanor. Darcy was a lot younger than him, blue eyes, thick dark hair. And the way she looked at her fiancé… What he'd give to have a woman look at him like that again.

Again?

His heart kicked.

He shot a glance at June, worried that something might have been revealed in his features, but her attention was on Darcy, who was setting mugs of coffee on the table. Jesse returned his attention to Darcy—there was something about her looks that made him uncomfortable.

Rafe cursed after hearing June out. He surged to his feet and began pacing the kitchen, anger, desperation powering his movements. Darcy watched him, concern growing in her eyes.

"To convince someone to give up their own child?" Rafe shook his head. "I can't believe even Samuel and Fargo would stoop *so* low." He spun round. "And to think I actually *thanked* Fargo and Samuel for their help!" He raked a hand through his thick black hair.

"That baby boy looked so much like the picture I had of Devin. Same hair color, same eyes—I believed in my heart it was my son. Why would they do this?"

"Maybe to shut you up, Rafe," June said. "Maybe they felt you were getting too close to the truth, and whatever the truth is, it must be detrimental to them. Perhaps they figured if you believed Aiden was Devin, then you'd be quiet, leave town."

"*If* what Tyler says is true," Jesse cautioned.

Rafe nodded. "DNA will either prove or disprove his story." He turned to June. "Have you informed the FBI?

They've been involved in the kidnapping investigation from the get-go."

"I'll be speaking to Agent Hawk Bledsoe when he returns to Cold Plains tomorrow. I'm going to invite him to the safe house to speak to the occupants. I've sheltered them from law enforcement until now, but Tyler's story is just unreal. This whole thing is getting way too dangerous."

Both Darcy and Rafe stared at June in silence.

She rubbed her face. "I'm not giving up, if that's what you're thinking."

Darcy reached out and took June's hand. "Hey, it's okay. Samuel and his flock are getting real edgy." She glanced at her fiancé. "Rafe and I are worried this place could turn into a Waco any day now."

Rafe nodded, drew up a chair, reseated himself at the table.

"You okay, June? You look tired."

"Fine." She said it a little too crisply.

"You should take a break, get some rest."

"Listen to the doctor, June," Darcy said with a kind smile.

Concern wormed into Jesse. June *did* look more drawn and pale than usual, and her hands were still shaking slightly, although she tried to hide it, as she was doing now, by clutching them both tightly around her mug as she sipped her coffee.

She ignored the concern, changing the subject. "Now we know why Bo Fargo called off his search for the kidnapper," she said. "Without Tyler, there's no one to prove Aiden was not your son."

"Then where *is* my son?"

"All we can do is keep looking, Rafe," Darcy said. "We can't give up. Just like I'm never going to give up the search for my real mother."

Rafe smiled, his affection tangible as he looked at his fiancée.

At least they had each other, thought Jesse as a pang of

loneliness speared into his chest. And the sudden ache, the sense of aloneness was so sharp, so real, that Jesse thought he couldn't possibly have a child or a wife in his life—or else he wouldn't feel like this, would he?

"Have you found anything new in the search for your birth mother, Darcy?" June was saying.

"I took the digitally enhanced image of Jane Doe, murder victim number two, back to my adoptive mother's town of Horn's Gulf. I showed it to anyone who'd look, but no one could verify Jane Doe was Catherine George. I just wish I could confront Samuel, and ask if he is my father, and if Catherine is my mother, which of course is out of the question." Darcy sipped her coffee. "I can't help thinking that if I go and look at the area where they found Jane Doe's body, I might learn something."

"Her body was found four years ago, Darcy," Rafe said. "There won't be anything there now."

"Maybe the killer goes back," she said. "Maybe a dog like Eager could find evidence of him visiting the site."

"I tell you what," said June. "As soon as I can find some time, we'll take my truck out there and search the site with Eager, look for human scent, any articles that might have been dropped by someone."

"Are you serious?" said Darcy.

"Sure I am." June glanced at Jesse. "Jesse will help."

"Thank you so much. I can't thank you enough."

"You shouldn't have promised Darcy you'd search the old crime scene with her—you're just going to let her down," Jesse said as he drove back to Hannah's farm. The afternoon was segueing into evening, the sun lowering in the sky, the light growing balmy and gold. June was relieved to have Jesse behind the wheel. She'd developed a mother of a headache and it was making her vision blur.

"I don't feel like discussing it," she said quietly, drawing tactile comfort from the way Eager was pressed against her.

Jesse's jaw tightened. The silence in the cab grew heavy.

"They have a good relationship. They make a nice couple," he said abruptly.

June massaged her temples with her fingertips, trying to make the pain go away. "Yeah, they do. Why does it upset you?"

"It doesn't."

"Sounds like it does."

He said nothing. She glanced at him—his profile was strong, his hands tight on the wheel, his neck muscles tense. Then because it was irking her, she said, "Does *none* of this bring back anything, Jesse?"

"No."

Jesse turned onto Hannah's ranch road. Dust boiled behind the truck, red in the evening sun.

By the time they reached the cave house it was dark.

June shrugged out of her pack and dumped it in the hall. She bent down to untie her hiking boots.

"I still think it was ridiculous to offer your help in searching a four-year-old murder scene," Jesse said, kicking off his own boots.

"What's it to you, Jesse?" June snapped. "Why are you so damn uptight about me helping Darcy out? I felt bad for her, okay? That's all."

Jesse dropped his voice to a harsh whisper as he realized the house was quiet, its occupants likely sleeping already. "You volunteered *my* help, June."

"Don't help me, then." June locked the front door and started down the hall for her bedroom. "I don't need your help," she called over her shoulder.

"You're a bleeding heart, June," he said, following her.

"You can't help every single person out there, you know. You're going to het—"

"Oh, don't start with me again." She spun around in front of her bedroom door. "Why are you so angry with me all of a sudden?"

"I'm not angry at *you*." He kept his voice low, but couldn't keep the edge out of it.

"Well, you're doing a damn fine job pretending—" And it hit her suddenly. "Oh, wait, I get it. You're mad because I said I'm bringing in Agent Hawk Bledsoe tomorrow."

"You could have mentioned it to me."

"Why? So you can run away quickly?"

"Maybe I'm not ready to meet him."

She glared at him. "Yeah, maybe you'll never be *ready,* Jesse."

She turned her back on him and entered her room. But he blocked her from closing the door.

"June—"

Anger fired inside her. "Jesse, please, leave me alone. Leave the safe house. I don't care where you go. Just—"

He grabbed her shoulders suddenly and yanked her hard up against his body, crushing his mouth down onto hers. Desperation, pent-up frustration, everything that had been simmering in June unleashed in his arms with explosive and blinding passion.

She opened her lips under his, moving her mouth against his, feeling his rough stubble against her cheek, and suddenly nothing but the present mattered—no past, no future, just this moment. She fumbled urgently to pull his shirt out from his jeans.

Edging her into the room, kissing her deeply, his tongue tangling with hers, slick, hot, wet, urgent, Jesse kicked the door shut behind them and backed her toward the bed. She could feel the rapid beat of his heart against her chest, and she felt the bulge in his jeans pressing against her pelvis. Her world tilted, began to spin. Liquid heat speared between her thighs, and she wanted him, all of him, deep inside, as she'd never wanted a man before. She began to breathe so fast she thought she might faint. Buttons pinged and bounced on the stone floor as she ripped his shirt open. She angled her mouth, kissing him deeper, moaning softly as her hands explored the hard, muscled lines of his torso.

His skin was hot, smooth, supple. She felt the ridges of his scars under her fingertips, and June was unable to articulate a single thought as a wild and furious urgency mounted inside her. She needed to grasp onto what she could before the past intruded on the present, before it shattered the future. Before Jesse knew who he was.

He slid her shirt back over her shoulders, exposing her bra, her belly, and she quickly began to unbuckle his belt. She felt the backs of her knees bump against the side of the bed as he lowered her down onto it.

Chapter 9

June peeled Jesse's jeans off his hips, her world narrowed to nothing but this moment. The light from the fire in the cast-iron stove danced copper over Jesse's naked, bronzed body. He stilled as he stood above her, his chest rising and falling, his eyes dark with passion and just a little wild, his hair mussed from her hands. And in that moment June knew with her whole being she could love this man. A raw ache swelled in her to have him, hold him, know him. Keep him.

His gaze holding hers, he reached out and removed the hair tie from the end of her braid. He loosened her curls around her bare shoulders.

"I thought you were an angel when I came around in your bed, you know that?" he whispered. She undid her bra as he spoke, and her breasts swelled free, nipples tight.

He placed his large, calloused hands on her shoulders and guided her onto her back as he lowered himself over her. He cupped her breast, rasped a rough thumb over her nipple. Something tightened low in her belly.

She reached up and placed a finger on his lips. "Don't talk," she said. She didn't want to think, and talk made caution whisper darkly around the edges of her consciousness. She wanted to stay only in the present.

He undid her jeans, slid them down her hips. Then he kissed her mouth and June felt his hand exploring the curves of her breasts, sliding down her stomach, cupping her hard between her legs as his kiss deepened.

June's vision spiraled as he slid a finger up inside her. Then another. He massaged parts of her that made every nerve in her body scream. It made her shake. Her vision turned red, then black as a low moan built in her throat. He moved his fingers deeper into her. She couldn't go slow like this. She wanted him fast, wild, furious. Hard. She hooked her hand around the back of his neck, yanked him down, and she kissed him almost angrily, moving her tongue inside his mouth, arching her back, opening her legs wider, rotating her hips, needing to deepen the sensation. She could feel the roughness of fingers inside her, the pad of his thumb rubbing on her swollen, sensitive nub, and she grew searing-hot, wet, delirious with physical pleasure.

Jesse groaned with pleasure at her urgency, thrusting his hand deeper, as his hips moved against her body and his erection pressed hot and hard against her thigh. It drove her wild, past a point of no return, and June could not hold back a moment longer.

She dug her nails into his back, trying to grasp onto the pleasure, to make it last, but every muscle in her body went tight and still for a moment, and then she shattered with a soft cry as wave after wave of contractions rocked through her body.

Jesse's control cracked. As she was shattering under him, he forced her legs open wider with his thighs and entered her with a hard, long thrust to the hilt. She was hot as molten metal inside, and he could feel the aftershocks of her contractions rippling over the length of his erection as he moved inside her.

She arched up her hips, gasping as he sank deeper and her fingernails dug into his neck. He moved wildly, bucking, grinding into her, deep as he could. She groaned in pleasure, rotating her hips, meeting him for every hard thrust he made.

Heat began to build. His vision turned scarlet. He could barely breathe. Every nerve in his body felt exposed, tingling, singing, right down to the hot tip of his erection. Every frustration that had been building in him quivered to the surface of his skin until Jesse felt he was going to explode. His muscles tensed as his vision darkened and his eyes rolled back in his head, and with one final thrust he released into her.

Breathing hard, body slick with perspiration, Jesse slumped down beside June, holding her close as she kept her legs wrapped around him. And as he gradually softened inside her, a memory began to return, like fire, crackling softly at the edges of his mind. The flames grew louder, bigger, hotter, coming closer. He began to panic as the sound became a roar of cracking and popping and spitting wood as his house burned.

Jesse froze inside.

His heart began to thud all over again.

Not now, he thought. *Not right now.* But more images came fast, furious, slicing like a hot knife through his brain. He saw the woman again. This time he saw her face. She reminded him of Darcy. That's why being with Rafe and Darcy had made him so edgy, angry, earlier.

But why the burning rage?

The dark-haired woman smiled at him. Her eyes were large and sparkling blue. In the next sharp image she was wearing white. A bride. He was sliding a smooth gold wedding band onto her finger.

Oh, dear God. Sweat beaded along Jesse's brow.

He closed his eyes tight, holding on to June, not wanting to let her go, terrified of what these images might mean to him. To her.

He saw a gold band on his own finger and another image flashed through his head—the dark-haired woman, very pregnant. Jesse's hand was on her stomach.

She was smiling. Anna...no, Annie. His throat turned dry. Her name was Annie.

But then she was crying. He was looking at the dark-haired baby in his own arms...or was it Tyler's baby? No, not Tyler's—Annie's. His. Jesse tried to calm his breathing. It was all coming back—finally coming back. And he didn't like it. Not one bit. The memory pieces felt like bad snapshots, harsh colors, from a family album that didn't really belong to him, yet it did. And like a series of random snapshots they were confusing, still not a smooth, continuous picture.

Jesse saw himself on a horse, going away. Far away. There were mountains, snowcapped peaks all around. His horse was negotiating rocky trails and he was going into higher, wilder places in search of...peace, of...something he couldn't put his finger on. The woman—Annie—his wife's screams suddenly shattered the peace. Jesse could see fire again. The baby was crying, stuck somewhere in the dark, and the flames were coming. He felt terror grip his heart.

Then nothing. Just silence. Mountains. And guilt. Sickening black guilt. Fear rippled through Jesse. He'd done something to Annie, to the baby. He felt it in the core of his bones. Something bad had happened.

He fingered his naked ring finger and slowly he opened his eyes.

June was propped up on her elbow, watching his face. A fall of red hair curtained her cheek and firelight was soft on her alabaster features. Her eyes glimmered, and she smiled, a little tentatively at first, then it deepened. With surprise Jesse registered she had a dimple.

She could light up a room with that smile. His gaze drifted down to her breasts. The way she was propped up on her side deepened her cleavage and her nipples were dark rose.

He allowed his gaze to go lower. Her stomach was flat, muscles firm. The hair between her legs was the same color as the waves hanging soft over her slender shoulders. He began to stir somewhere deep and carnal all over again.

Her words sifted softly into his mind.

Jesse, please, don't touch me. I can't do this. It's not going to work. I have no idea who you are. You might have a family or something waiting for you.

He swallowed. He'd made a mistake, he'd overstepped the line. And now he had to end it, because Jesse knew with sharp and sudden clarity he could not continue this with June—he was married. And he could not do this to June until he fully understood his relationship with Annie and the baby boy in his memory. Or until he knew where they were now.

A sick wave of nausea crawled up his chest and into his throat. And he didn't like the bitter taste that came with it.

"What are you thinking, Jesse?" Her voice was soft, sexy. She trailed her fingertips along his waist, feathering the line of a scar.

"About you."

"They're like a map, your scars," she whispered. "A map to your past, carved with blood into flesh. If only I had the key."

As she fingered the scar on his waist, another image slammed through him: his face hitting dirt, the taste of sand in his mouth. He heard hooves thundering, saw the horns of a steer flash past his eye. Then it was gone. But the taste of dirt and blood in his mouth seemed to linger.

"I think I could love you, Jesse Marlboro." Her eyes gleamed with sudden emotion. "I wish you could be just him. Just Jesse."

Her words cut. He felt pain in his chest, so raw. And with sudden clarity he knew it *was* his name—Jesse. The engraved belt buckle had been a Christmas present from Annie. He could see himself opening it by the tree, her smiling as he did.

He felt sick.

Self-hatred twisted into him.

He got up, went into the bathroom and closed the door carefully behind him.

He stood in the darkness for a moment, feeling his heart pound, listening to the rush of blood in his ears. Another image of Annie came to him. She was on a horse, riding behind him with other people. They were single file on a rocky trail in the mountains. Her short hair gleamed almost blue-black in the sunshine. She wore a Western vest and boots. Her laugh was like a wild brook. Sunlight, happiness, sparkled in her eyes. Another image bisected the first. He and Annie making love in a tent. In the mountains, *his* mountains. As abruptly as the vision had come, it was gone, like another night critter scurrying into the dark alleys of his brain.

Jesse flicked on the bathroom light and went to stand over the basin. He stared at his naked body in the mirror. There was no doubt about it, he'd been beaten up in the past, and the history of violence was written in a map of scars all over him, as June had said. His skin gleamed with perspiration and sweat beaded his lip. His eyes looked crazed. He turned on the tap and splashed ice-cold water over his face.

As he did, another memory washed over him. Adrenaline

was pounding through his blood, it was hot, a cowboy hat was on his head, a rope swinging in his hand. Muscles burned and hooves thundered on hard-packed dirt.

Steer wrestling.

It hit him with the weight of a hammer—he used to wrestle steers. He'd been gored, stomped on by his horse. But…it felt distant, further away than the memories of the dark-haired woman, the baby. This memory came from a more distant and youthful past. A wilder past.

Jesse peered intensely into the eyes that stared back at him from the mirror.

My Jesse with the blue eyes. He recognized the voice as his mother's, from way, way back. He glared harder at his own image, trying to dig further, unearth the secrets still buried in his head.

Jesse swore viciously to himself.

Think, dammit, think!

What did he know about himself? He liked physical action, adrenaline. He abhorred confined spaces, needed the great outdoors. He'd hunted poachers.

He rode horses and had wrestled steers. He slept often under stars.

He'd married a woman named Annie, with laughing blue eyes, and there'd been a child.

Suddenly another image hit him. He was fighting with Annie—they were yelling at each other, really going for it. Jesse felt the rage of the memory in the muscles at his neck, in the clench of his fists on the basin. Annie was crying. Then suddenly they were having sex again—wild, hot, angry. Guilt hammered down on the image, black and ugly.

Jesse! Jesse! Help!

She was screaming suddenly, locked somewhere in his head, the fire raging around her. His fault. But instead of helping her and the screaming baby, he was riding away, on a horse. Far away from her, from the baby.

His mind went blank. He was breathing so hard he felt he might hyperventilate

He slammed his hands down on the edge of the basin, hung his head down, trying to slot the disparate pieces together.

But all he could think of was June, lying naked in the bed on the other side of this door, and how much he wanted *her*.

His eyes burned.

He was falling in love with her. Absolutely no doubt about it. But he had another life and in it was a woman named Annie.

So why was he here in Cold Plains, with no ID, just a pack on his back and the name Samuel Grayson in his mind?

Was Annie in Cold Plains somewhere? With their child? Was she trapped by Samuel and his cult?

He had to find out.

And he had to do it without June.

Jesse needed to know how Annie fitted into his life before he could even begin to think again of June. He had to walk away, now, and it cut him to the core. Because he knew it was going to hurt her. And it was going to hurt him.

He'd hike out of Hidden Valley into Little Gulch before dawn broke. From Little Gulch he'd find an FBI field office. He'd ask the feds to help trace his identity.

If he'd done something terrible to Annie, he *had* to have done it for a reason, because Jesse couldn't believe he was an evil guy, a bad guy. Sometimes, he thought, a good person could be forced into an act the law might not deem justifiable. And sometimes the legal system itself was morally indefensible.

With a heavy and painful heart, Jesse took a quick shower.

He stepped out of the bathroom with a white towel around his waist.

June was lying on her back on the bed, a sheet covering her body. Her hair was splayed out in a soft halo of waves on the white pillow. She'd fed more logs onto the fire and the room glowed orange. Her eyes were wide, skin pale, and a nervous tension tightened her features as she watched him exit the bathroom.

"Are you okay?" she said quietly.

He raked his hand over his damp hair. "June...I..."

Christ, I don't know how to say this.

She sat up, gathering the sheet tightly around her chest, and he hated what he was about to do to her. He told himself he was not running away. He was doing this with the faint hope he could find his way back to being with her—if she'd still have him by then.

Taking a deep breath, he jumped.

"June, I need you to understand—" He swallowed. "I need to go away, leave the safe house. Now."

"Why?" Her eyes crackled suddenly, hands tense on the sheet, her face tight.

His heart hammered. Jesse came up to the bed and sat on the edge.

"I've decided to leave before sunup and hike over the mountains to Little Gulch. From there I'll find an FBI field office and ask them for help in tracing my ID."

She was silent for what seemed an eternity. Her eyes began to water.

"I...don't understand, Jesse. I thought you said you didn't want to involve the feds until—" It hit June suddenly and she sat up, stiff.

"You've remembered."

It wasn't a question.

"Not all of it. Just slices. But I need to fill in the rest. I have to find out why I am here. I…think someone I know, from my past, might be in danger in Cold Plains."

"Who?"

He reached out to touch her and she pulled away, got out of bed, wrapping the sheet tightly around her.

"June—"

"Who, Jesse!"

"I'm not sure."

"It's a woman, isn't it? Someone you're involved with."

He swallowed. Then nodded.

Her face went white as the sheet.

"What's her name?" Her voice came out hoarse.

"Annie," he said, bitterness filling his mouth, his eyes burning. "I…married her."

An almost imperceptible shock rippled through her body.

"June—"

She pulled back from his touch.

"I don't *feel* married. I have no ring." He hesitated. "We had a baby. I can remember a baby in the house."

Her eyes filled with moisture. A single tear shimmered down her pale cheek.

"Did you know any of this before…before—"

"Before I slept with you? No. I had snippets, but they made no sense. They suddenly seem to be slotting together."

"Do you know who you are, your name?"

"It is Jesse—the name on my belt. My surname still eludes me. I—I know things that I've done, June, not good things. They're just disjointed pieces, sensations, floating around my brain, and I still can't put them together in a whole picture. Which is why I'm going to ask the feds to help me."

"You were afraid of the FBI before. So why now?"

"Now there's you."

"I don't understand."

"Now I will take whatever knocks are coming, because I want to see if I can clear the way to be with you, June."

He reached for her hand, but June pulled away. She stared at him.

The hurt on his face was visceral. It cut like a knife through her stomach. She felt herself starting to shake inside. "Wait for Agent Bledsoe, please. He'll be here tomorrow. You can talk to him. You don't have to go."

"I can't be here with you. Not until I sort this out. I don't want to hurt you, June. So I'm going to get help."

June's world tilted on its axis. Maybe he was telling the truth—maybe he didn't know he had a wife and child before sleeping with her.

You need to give him the benefit of the doubt.

Which she hadn't given Matt. And it had killed him.

But it didn't change what had happened, or the way she felt. Or how wretchedly she hurt. But this was her fault—she'd let it happen. She'd allowed him to open the cracks in her heart. She made the decision to sleep with him, too.

You didn't know him, and he didn't know himself, yet you took the risk, anyway...

She struggled to breathe, and it took a few more beats before she could speak again.

"So you're just going to cut yourself off from me? From Cold Plains? What if there is someone in Cold Plains you came to save?" She heard the plea in her own voice, and she hated it.

"June, it's not like that."

"What's it like, then?"

"I can't save anyone until I know who it is I might have come here for."

A darker thought struck her.

"You do remember, don't you?" She stepped closer to him. "You recall exactly what terrible thing you did, and now you're fleeing from the law, before Hawk gets here." She inhaled shakily, going hot. "Is that what you were doing here in the first place, Jesse? Coming to hide from the law inside a cult? Is that why you had the *D* tattooed on your hip and carried no ID?"

"No!" He ground the word out through clenched teeth, and anger, dark and hard, twisted into his features.

A thin, cold fear trilled through her.

Be careful, June. He really could be dangerous. To you and to everyone in here. Especially if he's just remembered who he is and what he's done.

"Fine," she said guardedly, trying to sound vaguely calm while her insides were jelly, while her chest was bursting with anxiety and pain.

"I acknowledge this is my own fault, Jesse. I knew all along you might have a life that couldn't include me. I knew you might need to leave the minute you remembered what was waiting for you. I rolled the dice." Her voice quavered. "And I lost. I'm a big girl—I can handle it."

The anger on Jesse's face dissipated. Raw concern filled his eyes. And he almost imperceptibly leaned toward her, as if reaching out to her, as if every part of him wanted to touch, comfort. Hold on to her.

Tears pricked into her eyes and her throat ached with the effort of trying to keep it all bottled in. "Go," she said, very quietly.

He gathered his clothes, then stalled near the door. "I'll be gone before dawn."

She said nothing.

He opened the door, started to leave.

"Jesse?"

He spun around, anticipation—*need*—in his eyes.

"If you do anything that will hurt these people, jeopardize the safety of this house—"

"That's not who I am, June. You've got that wrong."

He waited, as if there might be some answer, something she could say to him, or do, that would change his mind, change everything.

She began to shiver.

"Go," she said again.

He stepped into the passage and the door snicked shut behind him.

Tears, silent, slid down her face.

June sank onto the bed and buried her face in her hands, and she allowed herself to sob like a small child. Every emotion she'd pent up for five years seemed to come out now in great big body-jerking spasms. She had not sobbed like this since she'd watched her little Aiden's casket being lowered next to his daddy's bigger one, since she'd heard the dark, damp sods of Washington earth thudding onto the lids, taking them away from her forever.

And when June stopped crying, she had no fuel left in the tank, nothing to shore her up, to keep going with the fight. Jesse had been the last, soft straw that had broken the back of her resolve and dropped her to utter rock bottom. She curled up in a tight fetal ball on top of the bed, and felt empty. Nothing. Just blackness.

Jesse opened the door to one of the spare bedrooms, planning to change in there. He was surprised to feel Eager's wet snout nuzzling against his leg as he did so. Flicking on the light he saw Eager was all body-wiggle excited to see him.

Jesse ruffled the dog's fur wondering why he'd been locked in here. To the best of his recollection Eager had come into the hallway after he and June had hiked back to the safe house. The dog had then headed straight for the kitchen, in search of his water bowl and food, while Jesse had followed June to her bedroom.

Once he'd changed, Jesse checked his weapon and sheathed it back in his holster. He smoothed his hand over Eager's square head. "You'd better stay in here, bud. I don't want to be letting you out if this is where your handler wants you, big guy."

He closed Eager into the room, then went into the kitchen. It would be another long hike and he'd need to take water, some food. He should probably eat something now, too, although he had no appetite for anything. *Focus,* he told himself. He was on a mission for the whole truth of his life. It was an obstacle he needed to conquer if he wanted any chance in hell of finding his way back to June. But his heart grew even heavier at the thought.

If he did have a wife and child, he had responsibility, and Jesse knew in his gut he was not a man to shirk that.

Nor was June a woman who would take a man into her life under those circumstances, even if she loved him.

The kitchen was dark, but light from a waning moon outside painted the valley silver through the big living-room windows. Small clouds scudded across the moon, and a wind was making the trees sway. It looked like another storm front brewing—not an ideal time to set out into the backcountry.

As Jesse reached for the light switch in the kitchen, a movement outside caught his eye. His hand stilled. The shadow moved again and his pulse quickened.

Leaving the switch, he moved quietly across the dark kitchen and crossed the living room to the big window, staying carefully to the side. Outside, partially hidden by the shadows of a pine tree, was a human figure. Jesse's blood began to thrum with adrenaline.

The figure stepped out from the shadows and into a puddle of moonlight. Jesse saw pale hair.

Molly.

She was talking into a radio.

Quickly, he moved to the front door and opened it quietly. He heard a voice, male, deep, crackling over the radio: "How long is this tunnel? Over."

Molly keyed her radio. "If you've got radio reception again, you're almost at the end," she said quietly. "Once you exit the tunnel, you need to cross a wooden boardwalk and—" Molly froze like a deer in headlights as she caught sight of Jesse.

He barreled out of the front door, and she screamed as he grabbed her arm.

He snatched the radio from her hand, his fingers digging into her upper arm.

"What in hell do you think you're doing?" Jesse growled.

The male voice crackled over the radio now in Jesse's hand. "Okay, we're out of the tunnel now—can see the boardwalk ahead. Take cover, we're coming in."

Jesse heard a click.

Both he and Molly spun around.

June stood at the safe-house door, shotgun stock to her shoulder. In this pale lunar light she looked ghostly, eyes dark holes.

"Let her go, Jesse." Her voice was strange.

"June—this is—"

Her finger curled around the trigger. "Give that radio to Molly and let her go."

He released Molly, but kept the radio.

Molly ran to June's side.

"You bastard." June spat the words at him. "You played me. You, Samuel, Fargo, Kittridge—you set me up and I fell for your stranger story, your charisma, just like they all fall for Samuel's stories. Your amnesia was a ploy to get me to bring you to the safe house, wasn't it? So you could figure out what we were doing. You absolute sick bastard." Her voice caught. "What's worse, I slept with you. Was sex a good bonus?"

Jesse knew *exactly* what June was feeling right now—he could taste the bitterness of betrayal in his own mouth. An overwhelming remorse filled his body...and it hit him, square between the eyes.

Annie had betrayed him. She'd slept with another man.

"It's not what it looks like, June. I saw—"

Molly grabbed June's arm. "He was telling two henchmen on the radio how to find the safe house! You heard it yourself, June. You saw the radio in his hand," Molly said urgently. "They're almost here! It's his fault. *He's a mole.*"

Jesse set the radio down on the ground and held his hands out to his sides, tension thrumming through him.

"Molly's lying. She's the traitor. You've got to get inside, get to safety. Now."

Her mouth flattened. "I'm not going to fall for you again. Once a mistake—twice makes me a fool."

But as she spoke, a thudding of boots sounded along the boardwalk.

"June—get inside!" Jesse yelled. "They're here!"

Molly darted off into the dark bushes.

June swung her weapon to the source of the sound. Gunfire cracked through the air. Then everything seemed to continue in slow, sick motion. Jesse saw June stumble backward against the doorjamb. The shotgun fell to her feet. Her hand went to her chest. She seemed frozen in time for a moment, then slowly she slid down the doorjamb and crumpled into a heap on the threshold.

Chapter 10

Jesse raced toward June just as the two henchmen emerged from the shadows. One of the men fired and a bullet buzzed like a hot hornet past his ear.

He flung himself to the ground, rolling off the edge of the patio into the creek bed as another bullet *thwocked* into the trunk of a tree beside him, shooting out shards of wood.

Jesse reached for his sidearm. His heart was hammering, every sense and reflex heightened by adrenaline. He could scent moss, loam. Creek water was cold on his leg. He inched carefully up and peered over the edge of the patio.

A bullet zinged off rock and an image burst sharply into his mind; of another time when he'd been cornered and shot at. In an instant Jesse knew what that time was—he'd come across signs of poachers in the Wind River Mountains. They'd killed and field-dressed an elk and packed out the meat, leaving flies buzzing around the carcass in a field of wildflowers. He'd tracked them for two days, finally coming upon their camp near evening. But the father and son had ambushed him.

They'd killed his horses, taken his weapons. He'd escaped, badly injured. But he'd survived in the Wind River Mountains for three weeks before hiking his way out.

And with that memory came a whole tumbling series of others—and Jesse knew what he was. A warden for the Wyoming Department of Fish and Game—a wilderness cop who owned a ranch in the Wind River foothills. The knowledge fired his resolve. It fed a sense of righteousness and dogged determination, of *duty* into his blood.

As he edged up to see over the patio again, more images, fueled by intense adrenaline, burned into his brain.

He'd taken the warden job after Annie had cheated on him and become pregnant. After she'd given birth to a son, Jesse had left her and the infant on his ranch and gone into the mountains, searching for a way to deal with the possibility that Annie's baby belonged to another man, searching for a way to handle the pain of betrayal, a way to move forward with his wife.

Another bullet zinged past him and he saw the two men running in a crouch toward the safe-house door.

What are they going to do? Kill all the sleeping occupants of the safe house, including the children?

Jesse took careful aim, fired on the first henchman.

The man stalled, stumbled sideways, then hit the ground hard. The second man made it to the door. Jesse fired on him, hitting the doorjamb and splintering wood as the man clambered over June's body and ducked inside.

Jesse scrambled onto the patio and raced in a crouch to June's side, gun in hand. Relief punched through him when he saw her eyes flicker.

She's alive.

But terror climbed onto the back of his relief as he saw a

pool of blood, black in the silver moonlight, glistening on the floor beside her shoulder.

"June!"

"Go..." she whispered hoarsely, grabbing his shirt. "Please, Jesse, *go save them!*"

He hooked his hands under her arms, pulling her to cover.

"Leave me, dammit! It's a flesh wound. I—I'll apply pressure. Just don't let me lose them, Jesse. *Please.*" Tears gleamed on her cheeks. "Get the children first, Jesse."

Conflict warred inside him. In his memory he heard Annie's baby screaming, and he heard the fire coming.

"Don't make it all worth nothing, Jesse."

He removed her handgun, placed it in her hand. She clutched her other hand over the wound in her shoulder.

"Hang in," he whispered. "I'm coming right back for you."

He ran along the outside of the cave house to a window on the far side. He broke it, kicked glass free, climbed through and rushed first to the nursery where Lacy, the twins and Tyler's baby were still sleeping. Tyler was in another room with Brad. Davis was in yet another. Sonya, he knew, shared a room with Molly and Brad's mom, Tiffany. Jesse couldn't reach them all in time.

Get the children first, Jesse.

As he entered the nursery, Jesse could hear Eager barking madly. Then he heard a woman's scream.

Panic stabbed into his heart.

Lacy was sitting up in bed, roused by the noise.

"What's happening?" she said.

"Henchmen."

"They *found* us?"

"Get your kids and Tyler's baby, Lacy. Take them and go out the window in the games room. It's broken. Keep the children quiet. Stay hidden in the woods until I come find you."

He raced down the passageway. Davis was coming out of

his room. He was carrying a shotgun and he'd already met up with Brad and Tyler, who had freed Eager. Brad was holding him by the collar.

"Henchman got inside," Jesse whispered.

"My baby—"

"It's okay, Tyler. Lacy has him. She's hiding with him in the woods. You've got to stay here and help me get this guy, understand?"

The sound of a woman's scream reached them again.

"That way," he whispered. "Sonya's room."

Brad pressed himself against the wall on one side of Sonya's door. Tyler stood on the other.

"Davis, you stay right behind me."

Jesse kicked the door open.

Sonya screamed again. She was trying to fight off the henchman with a baseball bat. The henchman swung around as he heard Jesse enter, and Sonya took the gap, crashing the bat down hard across his shoulders. The man grunted, stumbled, then buckled to the ground in pain. Eager burst past Jesse and attacked the man, biting into his leg.

The man tried to kick Eager off. Jesse grabbed the man as Davis got hold of Eager's collar and pulled him off.

The man's pant leg was torn and there was blood. His face was white with pain.

"I know him," said Tyler, staring at the fallen henchman. "He's Lumpy, Jason's friend, who came to make me give up my son. You bastard!" Tyler lunged for the man.

"Hold him back, Brad. This guy is not going anywhere."

Lumpy glowered at Jesse. "You're him, aren't you?" His voice was hoarse with pain. "You're the guy from the woods who killed Jason Barnes."

"Tyler, Brad, get him up," Jesse said, holstering his Beretta. "Lock him in the utility room, watch him until I get back. Davis, you take the shotgun, go look for Molly outside."

Lumpy swore and then groaned in pain as they tried to lift him.

"I think she broke my ribs with the bat, man. I—I can't breathe."

Jesse raced back to where he'd left June.

He found her passed out against the wall, gathered her up into his arms and carried her quickly into her bedroom, which was warm from the fire. He lay her on the bed and flicked on the light. Memories, everything he knew about himself and his past, rushed like a wild stream through his head. The life-and-death situation, the kick of adrenaline, must have shocked it all back, and Jesse now knew exactly who he was—Jesse Grainger.

He knew what had happened to Annie and the baby. He also knew why he no longer wore a wedding band. And it was a promise he'd made to Annie on her deathbed that had brought him here to Cold Plains. Above all, Jesse was now certain there was room for June in his life, and here she was, slipping away from him.

He could *not* lose her now.

He could not let her die thinking he was evil, a traitor.

"June," he whispered, emotion burning in his eyes, panic licking through his stomach.

"Wake up, June. Stay with me."

She moaned, and her eyes flickered open. Relief punched through his chest. Jesse worked quickly to take off her shirt. There was an ugly gouge through the outside of the flesh on her upper arm. God, she was lucky—the bullet had only ripped through flesh.

"Sonya!" he yelled. "Tiffany!"

The two women came running. "Get me June's first-aid stuff! Get me a bowl of hot water, cloths. Hurry!"

June was delirious, moaning.

"Stay with me, girl, hang in. I love you, you know that? You're not going to get away from me now."

Jesse cleaned and disinfected her wound, his own basic first-aid training kicking in. He pulled the edges of skin tightly together with adhesive butterfly sutures from June's kit, and he bound her arm firmly with a bandage.

With a cool, damp cloth he wiped her face.

She opened her eyes.

"Hey," he said, his chest cramping with relief. "You're going to be okay. You got lucky—it's a flesh wound."

"The children—"

"Everyone is safe, June. We got the bad guys." He smiled.

But she was not looking right. He needed to get her medical attention. Sonya brought him a fresh shirt for June.

"Is she going to be okay?" said Sonya.

He nodded. "But I want to get her to the hospital."

"No." June's voice was hoarse as she grabbed his arm. "Not the hospital in Cold Plains. I can't go there, not after this attack. None of us can go into Cold Plains right now."

"June, your pulse is weak, something's going on with you—"

She shook her head. "It's just a flesh wound. I'll be fine." Confusion crossed her face suddenly. "Jesse—the radio in your hand. You were guiding those men in."

"No," he said gently. "It was Molly. I was in the kitchen when I saw her outside talking on the radio. I'd just grabbed it from her when you came out the door."

"She…can't be. Not Molly."

"I'm afraid so, June."

She frowned, a confused look entering her eyes.

"She must have infiltrated via your rescue system," he said. "My guess is that she didn't expect to arrive at a house outside of cell-phone range, and that the plan was for her to call in her location. But once here, she had no way of letting the men on the outside know where she was without blowing her cover. I believe that's why she hiked out to the end of the valley the other day, when she encountered the bears. She might have gotten enough of a signal to let them know the safe-house radio frequency, or they got lucky and tuned in."

"That means there could be more men coming, Jesse," she whispered.

He took her hand in his.

"Perhaps," he said. "But there's also a chance those two henchmen didn't have a chance to pass on information about the safe house."

Her eyelids fluttered closed and she sighed deeply.

"So…tired," she whispered. "So…very tired."

Jesse glanced at Sonya, who was standing to the side. She looked as worried as he felt.

"June?" he said, turning back to her.

Silence.

"I think she's fallen asleep," said Sonya.

"I'm going to fetch Dr. Black," Jesse said, standing up. "And then I'm going to get the FBI. Watch her, Sonya." Emotion choked his voice. "Don't let anything happened to her, and stay off the radios, okay? I'll tell the others to stand guard."

He took June's shotgun and several boxes of shells from the cabinet. Thrusting them into a pack, he hurried to the utility room where Molly Rigg and Lumpy Smithers were now being held.

He knocked on the door.

Tyler opened it. Jesse stepped in. The utility room was tiny, rock walls, stone floors, no windows, vented from above. Using June's climbing rope, the men had managed to tie both Lumpy and Molly—whom Davis had found not far from the safe house—to the heavy plumbing that ran along the bottom of one wall.

"Lumpy said he wants to talk to the feds," Davis said quietly in Jesse's ear. "He's broken up about Samuel wanting him to leave Jason to die. I think he's done being a Devotee. Agent Hawk Bledsoe might actually get something concrete out of him he can use against Samuel."

Jesse glanced at Molly. Her face was tight with rage. He doubted she was going to break in a hurry.

"I'm going to fetch Rafe Black and Agent Bledsoe," he told them. "Once Dr. Black has looked at June, he can take a look at Lumpy here. Have you got a cell phone I can use to contact Bledsoe?"

"Take mine." Davis handed Jesse his phone.

"Thanks. I'll call ahead for Black to be ready to roll as soon as I get there. I'll call Bledsoe on my way down."

"Both their numbers are in my contact list," Davis said. "If you go into town via the south trail you'll actually hit Bledsoe and Carly's ranch before you hit town."

As Jesse left the room Molly yelled at him: "You sick SOB—Samuel will find us! His men will find us! This place, June, they're the evil among us. She and this house go against everything the Devotees are trying to build. She's like a cancer!"

Her voice faded as Jesse made his way down the stone passage, urgency mounting in him.

But, as he went, Jesse tried to temper his anger at the kid. She'd been indoctrinated by a sick sociopath. Yes, she was dangerous, but she needed help, too. She was also a victim of Samuel's.

Just as his young brother-in-law, Michael, was a victim.

And Jessie knew now that he'd promised Annie on her deathbed to come to Cold Plains and get Michael out.

When he stepped out the door with his twelve-gauge and his pack, the sky was already black and low with clouds, and rain was beginning to spit. Thunder rumbled in the hills.

By the time Jesse was out of the tunnel and the canyon on the other side, the rain was coming down hard and the wind was whipping debris down from the treetops. He moved fast along the south trail with the aid of a headlamp and his GPS. He was now certain of who he was. He trusted his law-enforcement training and his experience in the wilderness, and his sense of purpose was clear and fierce, as was his sense of justice.

He had a brother-in-law somewhere down in that town—he could see lights through the rain and trees now. His duty was to keep a vow to his deceased wife—a woman he'd always cared for but had struggled to love since her infidelity. And now there was June, a woman he *did* love, her well-being hanging by a thread.

Thunder crashed and a bolt of lightning forked across the black dawn over Cold Plains; like an omen, thought Jesse, because the wrath of justice was going to strike down Samuel Grayson and his perfectly evil little community. Thunder growled again and echoed into the mountains. Jesse could now make out lights from what must be Hawk and Carly Bledsoe's ranch house. He bent into the wind, face wet, muscles burning as he began to jog down the last stretch of meadow trail that led to the ranch. Rain was pelting horizontally at him as he banged on the door.

More lights went on inside the house.

The door swung open.

A tall, muscular man with sandy-blond hair and brown eyes stood in the doorway. The man's hand went to his hip where he had a pistol holstered.

"Agent Hawk Bledsoe?" said Jesse.

Hawk identified himself, eyes narrowing.

"My name is Jesse Grainger." And it felt damn good to say it. "I've just come from the safe house run by June Farrow—she's been shot. They've been attacked by henchmen."

Hawk motioned him inside.

Quickly, Jesse explained who he was, why he'd come and how the two men had attacked the cave house. "One man went down when I returned fire. The other is being held captive in a utility room along with the Devotee mole."

As Jesse explained that he was on his way to fetch Dr. Rafe Black, two men and two women appeared behind Hawk. He introduced one of the women as Carly, his wife, and the others as his team of FBI agents assigned to the Samuel Grayson investigation.

"I mapped my route from the cave house," Jesse said, handing Hawk his GPS. "All you have to do is follow the waypoints. When you go into the rock crevasse, it narrows to what appears to be a dead end. Move the creepers aside, and you'll expose the opening to the cave with a tunnel leading off the back. Go through the tunnel until it pops out into Hidden Valley on the other side. The cave house is at the end of a boardwalk that leads from the tunnel."

Carly was pulling on a rain jacket as Jesse spoke. "I'll take you to Dr. Black's in my SUV," she said. "Telephone lines and the cell tower are down because of lightning strikes."

She flung open the door and, pulling up her hood, began to run through the pelting rain to a vehicle. Jesse followed her.

Thunder clapped as she opened the driver's door, her face white in the simultaneous flash of lightning. The lights inside the house dimmed and flickered. Urgency kicked through Jesse.

By the time they pulled up outside Rafe and Darcy's place,

water was running in rivers over the roads. Jesse banged on the doctor's door.

Rafe flung open the door, eyes sharp with adrenaline. "Did you find Devin?"

"No, Rafe, not yet. It's June—she's been shot. It's a flesh wound but I'm worried about her. Something else is going on—can you come to the safe house?"

The disappointment in the doctor's eyes was keen, but he barely blinked as he hurried to pull on some gear and grab his kit. Darcy stood in the lit doorway watching them pull off.

Tires skidded on mud as Carly struggled to get the SUV as far up a logging track as the vehicle could go in order to make the hike shorter.

"That's one good thing about this weather," said Jesse as they climbed out of her vehicle, pulling up their hoods. "There's no one around to see us."

"Good luck," Carly called behind them as they started up the trail. "Be careful!"

The concern in her voice was sharp, and Jesse felt a sense of kinship, of being part of a greater team, something he'd been missing for a long, long time.

Carly left her headlights on, lighting their way until they disappeared into the trees.

Rafe, Jesse noted, was fit, and although remaining cautious in wilderness terrain in the dark storm, the two of them moved quickly.

It was not long before they were at the cave entrance.

Jesse watched as Rafe finished suturing June's wound. Hawk and his team had arrived ahead of Jesse and Rafe, and were now busy with the captives in the utility room.

"Does she need to go to the hospital?" Jesse asked the

doctor, still worried about June's sheet-white complexion and the deeply bruised look under her eyes.

"I'm fine," June murmured.

"I'm asking the doc, not you," Jesse said with a big, forced smile, thinking that even her voice seemed flat, listless. And he didn't like the way she was avoiding eye contact with him.

He had to tell her, now, about who he was. She still didn't know.

Rafe packed up his medical kit. "I'll be back in a while to check on you, June," he said as he worked with practiced calm, "after I take a look at Lumpy Smithers. Sounds like he might have broken a few ribs. And I'm going to check in on Tyler's baby while I'm here."

Lacy, the twins and the baby were safely back in the house, and Jesse heard the ache in Rafe's voice and knew he was thinking of his own son. He followed Rafe out of the room and took him aside in the kitchen.

"Rafe, what's really going on with her?"

Rafe set his bag on the counter. "June has been putting herself under extreme mental and physical stress, day in and day out for over three months now. I think her system is just giving in under the strain. I wouldn't rule out critical-incident stress, either. She might need counseling herself, Jesse. More than anything, June needs to rest."

"I don't think she knows *how* to stop."

Rafe nodded. "She needs help, Jesse. She needs someone to take over for her for a while, and insist she put her feet up."

Jesse snorted. "Like June is going to allow anyone to take over and give orders."

"Someone has to." Rafe shook his head and picked up his bag. "I've told June to take it easy, but she's dogged in her drive to help others. Sometimes I think she's just as trapped by it all as the Devotees are by Samuel."

"It's because of her husband and child."

"I know," Rafe said. "And I get it. I'm just as driven to find my own son as she is to set right the perceived wrongs of her past."

Emotion burned in Jesse's chest as he watched the doctor go down the passage toward the utility room. Rafe had summed it up. He was a good man and an astute doctor. There were a lot of good people mixed up in this net of Samuel Grayson's.

Jesse opened the door to June's room.

"Hey," he said gently.

She turned her head on the pillow away from him, and something dropped like a stone in his stomach.

He came up to the bed, sat down on the edge and tried to take her hand. She moved it away, still not looking at him. Eager, however, nuzzled against Jesse's leg, clearly worried about his mistress. Jesse stroked his soft fur instead.

"Hawk Bledsoe has things under control," he told her. "He's hopeful he can get Lumpy to give him something on Samuel."

She said nothing.

Exasperation, worry, whispered through him.

"June, we're going to win this."

She turned her head, looked at him. His heart sank at the pallor in her face, the vacancy in her eyes.

"We?" she said quietly.

"Yes, June. You and me."

"You're wet," she said, looking a little confused again.

He snorted. "It's raining cats and dogs out there, worse than the night you found me. June, listen—"

"Lacy and the twins, the baby?"

"They're all fine. We saved *everyone*."

Her eyes moistened and she bit her lip.

"June, I have something to tell—"

Hawk gave a knock and entered the room. Jesse cursed silently.

"You doing okay, June?" said the agent.

She nodded. "Thanks for coming, Hawk. I've been trying to reach you."

He smiled as he came forward, his brown eyes guarded but friendly. The man exuded a cop's air of authority and confidence.

"You can thank Jesse," said Hawk. "Landlines and the cell tower went down in the storm. Jesse hiked down the south trail and came banging on our door at the ranch in the thick of it all. Carly drove him down to get Doc Black while we headed straight here using his GPS mapping."

June frowned, glanced at Jesse. "*You* fetched Hawk?"

"Looks as though we might get Lumpy Smithers to turn on Mayor Rufus Kittridge and Monica Pearl in a plea bargain," Hawk interjected. "Lumpy was close to Jason Barnes and he feels betrayed by Samuel wanting him to let Barnes die. If we can charge Kittridge and Pearl, Samuel's two militia leaders, we might finally get something from them to pin on Samuel. It would help if we could locate Samuel's twin, Micah. He was the one who started this ball rolling, saying he could help us take his brother down."

"What happened to him?" asked Jesse.

Hawk gave a half shrug. "He vanished into thin air. No leads on him at all. Perhaps Samuel got to him first."

"What about Molly Rigg?" June said, trying to edge herself higher up to sit back against the pillows.

"As tough-talking as that kid is, once we start interrogating her, I have a feeling she's going to give."

"Promise me you'll allow Molly access to counseling, deprogramming, legal advice, before you interrogate her," June said, and Jesse's heart hurt for her—even in her weakened state she was still worried for others.

"Of course," said Hawk. "I've seen firsthand with Mia what a cult can do to a loved one, and how deprogramming can work like a switch—I believe in what you do, June, can't thank you enough, none of us can."

"Did Sonya show you around the safe house?" said June.

"She did—I'm impressed. And from what Lumpy and Molly are saying, no one beyond the two of them now knows the location of the cave house—it's still secure to the best of my knowledge." He turned to Jesse, paused, a grave and businesslike look entering his already-serious features.

"When you're ready, Jesse, we've got some procedural stuff to go through with you."

Jesse nodded.

He'd shot and killed two men in self-defense since his arrival in Cold Plains. One of them was lying dead outside right now. There would be consequences that would need to be legally addressed, statements made and taken.

He waited for Hawk to exit, then he got up and closed the door, desperate for a moment of privacy with June.

"Jesse," June said quietly, turning her head away from him as if she couldn't bear even to look at his face. "I need to be alone."

He came and sat back down on the bed beside her.

"Please," she said.

"I'm not going anywhere, June. Not anymore. I remembered. Everything."

She turned her head, met his gaze.

"Everything?" she whispered.

"I know who I am, June."

A nervousness crept into her eyes.

Emotion suddenly crackled hard and fierce into his chest, and he took her hand in his. "And I *know* there is a place in my life for you."

Chapter 11

June met his gaze. His energy was palpable, his eyes fierce with a kind of fervor she'd not seen in him before, and she was suddenly afraid of what he was going to say. She'd wanted so desperately to allow herself to love him, but in taking the risk she'd seen just how raw she still was about loss, and how much she could still be hurt. June wasn't sure she could ever give herself wholly over to someone again, or if she even wanted to try. The cost of losing again was too high for her.

"What do you mean, 'a place in your life'?" Her voice came out hoarse. She felt shaky. Her shoulder throbbed. Part of her suddenly wanted to flee.

"June—" His hand tightened around hers—large, calloused, capable, protective. And threatening. Her pulse quickened and her skin felt hot.

"My name *is* Jesse—Jesse Grainger. I know weapons, wildlife, bears, because I work as a game warden in north-western Wyoming. I came to Cold Plains because of a promise I made to my wife—"

"So you *are* married," she said flatly, not wanting to hear more.

A muscle pulsed at his temple. Time seemed thick, slow. And June could see pain in his eyes. As exhilarated as he was in rediscovering who he really was, June could see the memories were not easy for him.

"I'm a widower, June."

She stared at him, heart beginning to hammer.

"My wife, Annie, died from injuries sustained in a fire."

"How?" she whispered.

He glanced away for a moment, and swallowed. June's heart squeezed and she slid her hand along the bed, tentatively touching her fingertips to his thigh, just making the barest of physical connections, yet afraid, still, of what he was about to say, afraid to dare to believe. And hating herself for the whisperings of exhilaration she was beginning to feel in the face of his loss.

"I'd been doing some renos to our ranch house. I'd put in the wiring myself and there was a problem with the electrics. The wiring caught fire and the blaze spread very quickly through the house. Our son was sleeping in a room at the back of the house." Jesse hesitated. "He...died in the fire."

Her heart began to pound, loudly, in her ears, images of her own son drumming through her mind.

"Annie tried to save him, but couldn't reach the room in time. Firefighters managed to pull her out of the house alive, but she succumbed to her injuries and died in the hospital two days later."

"What was your son's name?"

"Cameron. I was in the mountains when it happened. I was contacted via radio, and managed to make it back in time to be at Annie's bedside when she passed."

Silence trembled thickly in the air.

"I'm so sorry, Jesse." June placed her hand on his thigh.

He sat still for a while, his pulse throbbing at his neck.

"When did this happen?"

"Four months ago." He inhaled deeply. "The worst thing, June, is the guilt I feel for not having been there. That's the guilt that has been dogging me even though I couldn't recall why. I feel bad because of it. If I hadn't been out in those mountains, I might've been able to save them. And I'm weighed down by the fact it was my wiring that started the fire. I killed them, June."

"Jesse, you can't blame yourself. You were doing your job—"

"I *can* blame myself. June, listen to me—" He put his head back and stared at the ceiling, as if gravity might hold back some of the emotion suddenly gleaming in his eyes.

"I had unresolved issues with Annie," he said quietly. "I hadn't found a way to love Cameron yet. I wasn't even supposed to be in those mountains for so many days, weeks, months at a time. But I'd taken the warden job expressly to be away from Annie and the baby, from the ranch, to figure it all out. To find a way to deal with Annie's infidelity and the fact that Cameron was probably not my child."

"Oh, Jesse." June pushed herself higher onto her pillows.

He leveled his gaze at her.

"I needed the time to decide whether I wanted to go the DNA–paternity test route, or just to accept and love Cameron as my own. It wasn't his fault, and he was a beautiful child. But this idea of never knowing haunted me. And I couldn't help thinking of what Annie had done to our marriage every time I looked at 'our' baby boy—he was fair with green eyes. Annie had blue eyes, like I do, and almost blue-black hair." He swallowed. "In fact, I realize now that Darcy reminded me of Annie. I couldn't figure out why it bothered me looking at her, why her affection for Rafe seemed to cut at me so badly. Why I envied their obvious love."

"Tell me about Annie," June said softly. "How did you meet her?"

He rubbed the dark stubble on his jaw. "Some years back, before I ever considered the game-warden position, I used to guide hunting trips on horseback. I'd take time out from my cattle ranch in the Wind River foothills—leave the place in the hands of a manager—and guide a few high-end trips each season. Annie came with her father from New York one year, and she fell in love with the mountains, with me. I think it was more the whole Wyoming-cowboy image that got her, the romance of the open sky, the big ranch, which has been in my family for four generations… Whatever it was, her attention was intoxicating… We married a year later and settled on the ranch. She kept up her freelance editing business, flying back to New York for business once or twice each year, in addition to other travel." He paused.

"It worked well for a time, June—things were looking good. But then Annie met up with an old flame on a social-media site, someone she'd known from school who'd always had a thing for her. This guy flew down to see her, and they met at a town over, in a hotel bar. I learned from another rancher that she'd been seen there with a guy, and that they'd stayed overnight at the hotel together. I confronted her about it—it led to a terrible argument. Apparently they had hot monkey sex… She said it was a mistake, said she was sorry, wanted me to forgive her. She claimed it was a last-fling kind of thing, something she'd needed to get out of her system."

Jesse cleared his throat. "I took it hard, June. It wasn't so much a blow to my ego as the fact I'm a one-woman kinda guy. Commitment is huge to me. We battled along for some months, sidestepping each other. She grew unhappy. I was unhappy." He stared at June's hand on his jeans and the brackets around his mouth seemed to deepen, as did the lines around his eyes. June's heart broke for him.

"I fell out of love," he said quietly. "It was that simple, and that complicated. All the affection, the passion, just fizzled to nothing. It was a heavy time, and then came the news of her pregnancy. I figured the timing was such that it could've been from her night with her old flame. Annie said it wasn't, but only a paternity test would prove either way. That's when the job of game warden came up. It's what I had trained for when I left school, back in the days when I was young and wild, and when I used to do things like steer-wrestling." He smiled sadly, and June suddenly loved him, so wholly that it scared the crap out of her. She cleared her throat.

"So you took the warden's job?"

He nodded. "Mostly because it took me away, out into the wilderness, alone, sometimes for weeks at a time. I wanted to think—just me, the horses, the mountains, the big skies. I wanted to find a way to forgive her, June. I *wanted* to love the baby as our own. But you know what really cut? I'd wanted kids, and every time I'd broached the issue, Annie had stalled, saying she wasn't ready. And there she was, giving birth, caring for what was possibly another man's son." He swore softly. "It messed with my head."

"Are you sure he wasn't yours, Jesse?"

"Deep down, yeah, I was convinced Cameron wasn't mine. I think I was just afraid to do a test because it would just prove it with finality, drive it home, and I'd have to deal with it. We'd both have to make decisions. If I didn't do the test, I could still believe. There was still a chance. And that's what I was trying to work through when news of the fire reached me."

There was pain in his face, in the way he held his shoulders, in the corded muscles in his neck. And June understood—it was lack of closure. Because he hadn't done the test, there would forever remain the chance his own son had perished in the fire. Closure was a tough nut to crack, and the need for it sometimes difficult to understand.

"You didn't want to do a test…after?" she said.

He snorted softly. "Why? To make my grief worse? To mourn less for little Cameron because he wasn't my blood? Knowing doesn't diminish the fact a baby died."

She placed her hand on his forearm where he'd rolled up his shirt. His skin was warm, his dark hair coarse, masculine.

"Why'd you come to Cold Plains, Jesse? What was the promise you said you made to Annie?"

He scrubbed his brow, then winced slightly as he connected with the stitches along his temple.

"I sat with Annie at her hospital bed, until the end. She was in a lot of pain, badly burned. She pleaded again for my forgiveness, and I told her she had it, that I understood."

"Do you…understand?"

"I'm old-school, June. I try to get it, to see myself in her shoes if the situation had been reversed—I can't."

"So you lied. You can't feel bad about that, Jesse. You told her what she needed to hear so she could pass peacefully."

He lurched to his feet, began to pace the room. He reminded June of a caged mountain lion. At first he had been caged by his amnesia. Now that he remembered, the bars were his guilt. She understood guilt. She knew how it could pervade and darken one's life—even if logic told you it was irrational. You might try to push the guilt down into the basement of your subconscious, but it was always there, lurking, coloring everything else, no matter what you did in an effort to assuage it…no matter how many people you rescued from cults. And June realized with a start she was thinking of her own guilt, of Matt and Aiden. And her own relentless drive to set right the wrongs of her past.

"On her deathbed," Jesse said, "Annie told me her younger

brother, Michael, had been sucked in by a cult in Cold Plains. She said the cult was run by a man named Samuel Grayson and that his followers were called Devotees. I didn't know until that day that it existed, or that Michael was even in Wyoming. Annie hadn't mentioned it to me, or asked for my help up until then, because we were dealing with the problems between us, and she hadn't wanted to impose her own family issues on me. But as she was dying, she begged me to try and get Michael out. Annie explained it would be difficult, and she was the one who told me about the *D* tattoos."

June frowned. "What's Michael's surname?"

"Millwood."

Her pulse kicked. "Mickey Millwood? Early twenties, sweet, gentle guy, dark hair, big blue eyes?"

"You know him?"

"It's a small town, Jesse, and I've made it my business to try and know the Devotees. Michael works at Samuel's water warehouse where Hannah does the bookkeeping three times a week."

He stared at her, neck muscles, jaw, tight.

"So Hannah has access to him?"

"Yes, she does. She's been looking out for Michael—she calls him Mickey. Hannah feels he's...vulnerable."

"He's dyslexic. And a little slow, yeah, I know. Annie told me he'd come to Wyoming because she was here, but before he could make it up to Wind River he came through Cold Plains, and he got sucked in by Samuel. Then he stopped all communication. She was worried sick about him, especially because of his disabilities."

Hatred for Samuel washed afresh through June and her blood began to pound hard, her old energy, her fire, returning, burning into her veins. "Samuel takes advantage of whatever he can," she said bitterly. "A kid like Michael is especially defenseless—it makes me sick to the gut what Samuel's doing."

"I came to get him out, June. I vowed to Annie I would, if it's the last thing I did. That's why I had such a sense of mission and a feeling that my presence here was somehow connected to the name Samuel Grayson. That's why the words *Devotee* and *cult* felt somehow familiar to me. My plan was to hike in with nothing but my backpack, posing as a down-and-out ranch hand looking for work. I figured I'd let drop that I had a bit of a gambling problem, which I hoped might provide an opening for Samuel, make him sympathetic to me. I thought I'd attend his seminars, make it look like I was a potential Devotee. I had the *D* tattoo done, like Annie had described, in case I needed it as a way to get in—I wasn't sure what to expect when I arrived."

He slumped back down onto the bed beside June and rubbed his hands over his face.

"It took me three months after I buried Annie and Cameron to get my act together to come here. I had to hire someone to take care of the ranch and I had to sort out my finances. I packed up everything and resigned my warden's position—I didn't know how long it might take to get Michael out, or how long I'd have to be here. It didn't matter. I had nothing else."

He paused.

"And I didn't expect to find you."

"Hey, it was *me* who found *you* down that ravine, remember?"

A sad smile toyed with the corners of his beautiful mouth. "Good thing I picked the side of the mountain with a search-and-rescue expert and her K9, huh?"

She laughed. It felt good, and it hurt, too—both emotionally and physically. Her hand went to the bandage on her arm.

"You okay?"

"Yeah, I'm fine. Really."

I'm a widower, June.

Those few words had tipped her world onto a different axis. But caution whispered through her. His loss was fresh. And she felt as though she was balanced precariously at the edge of a precipice—both exhilarating and terrifying.

"The last thing I ever wanted was to hurt you, June," he said, his deep indigo gaze holding her. "And I never expected to fall so hard for you."

She wanted to tell him she'd fallen for him, too. Much too hard and much too fast, but the words wouldn't come.

"It's why I tried to step away from what was happening between us when I recalled marrying Annie. But at the same time I didn't *feel* married—I needed to figure out what it all meant, and I couldn't do it here. I couldn't hurt you. And I couldn't be here without wanting to be with you."

He paused, took her hands. "Can you understand that?"

She nodded. "I can," she whispered. "It was my fault, Jesse—"

He touched his fingers to her lips and shook his head. "I shouldn't have allowed myself to feel for you, June. But now I'm glad I did. And when I've got Michael out, I want you to come with me, back to the Wind River, where you can rest awhile." His eyes were serious, sharp, his rugged features, resolute.

"Eager would love it there," he said very quietly.

June swallowed. He was telling her that he was free to love her, possibly even make a life with her in the foothills of the Wind River Mountains, on his ranch, if she'd come home with him.

Suddenly it all felt too fast. June began to panic at the thought of leaving what she knew—her mission. She was compelled to keep working for EXIT, saving victims from cults like Samuel's.

"How about it, June? Come back with me."

He was asking her to jump off the edge of that mental precipice upon which she so precariously balanced, and she honestly didn't know if she could risk loving so deeply and wholly again, and losing again. A second time would kill her—she knew this in her heart. A raw and irrational kind of terror swelled inside June's chest. Her mouth turned dry and the walls of the cave room suddenly seemed to press in on her.

Worry crawled into Jesse's eyes.

"It's beautiful country up there, June. Rolling hills. And in the distance, the jagged range of snowcapped peaks. It's free, wild, open. I have land, horses." He paused, concern deepening in his features. "Do you ride?"

She fiddled with her wedding band, forcing herself not to glance toward the photo of Matt, Aiden and her on the dresser—to not think of the two ghosts that walked quietly and constantly at her side. But their presence was strong. They'd come to define who she was. They were the parameters of her life and she didn't know how to separate herself from them, or how to live without the specter of them.

Abruptly, June swung her legs over the side of the bed. She waited for a nauseating wave of dizziness and pain to pass, then got to her feet, a little wobbly.

"What're you doing, June?" Jesse said, standing up beside her, steadying her with a hand on her elbow. She moved out of his reach, walking over to the dresser where her firearm lay in its holster beside the framed photo—she stared at the image, the past swirling into the present and blurring the future.

"We need to go and get your brother-in-law out," she said, reaching for the holster and strapping her weapon to her hips. "It's time to pull Hannah out, too. It's getting too dangerous for her—I'm worried that as soon as Samuel learns his henchmen aren't coming back, and if Hawk arrests the mayor, this whole place is going to blow. Hannah is going to get hurt, or worse."

"You're not going anywhere." His tone was brusque. "I promised Rafe I'd make you rest."

She turned to face him, could see the pain in his features, and her chest hurt. "Jesse, you can't make me do anything. You're not in charge here."

"You're running, June. You're running from yourself and you know it."

"I am not! This is triage. This is urgent. This is what I do!"

"You're afraid to let it go, aren't you? You want to hold on to your past like a shield."

"Jesus, Jesse—Hannah's and Michael's lives could be in danger."

"So is yours. You're going to kill yourself like this, June."

"Oh, please." She grabbed a rain jacket from her closet and realized her hands were shaking. He was right, and she didn't want to—*couldn't*—admit it. Her arm hurt like hell as she pulled on her jacket.

"June, I'm not asking you to give up your work for EXIT. Do you understand that?"

She hesitated, then zipped up her jacket.

"All I want is for you to rest, heal, and for us to spend some time together, get to know each other better. I thought you'd love it out there. It's who you are—that wilderness. It's who I am. We could make it work."

"It can't work, Jesse—I don't see how it can. My work keeps me mobile. And I won't give it up."

"June." His voice softened. "You can do this. You do live somewhere now, right?"

June stilled. Perspiration beaded on her lip in spite of the chill she felt in her bones.

"I have a small apartment in Portland," she said quietly. "It's my base at the moment, but I'm never there, Jesse—"

"Let my ranch be your base, temporarily. Baby steps."

She felt blood draining from her head. She felt hot. Anxiety, she thought. She was having a panic attack.

"I need to go."

"Sit down, June," he said firmly, taking her hands and leading her back to the bed. He seated himself beside her.

"Listen to me, and don't take this the wrong way. Don't say anything, either. I just want you to think about what I'm going to say." He inhaled deeply.

"You're trapped, June, not so much by your fight against cults, but by your notion that fighting them can change something about the past—that it can make right what happened to your husband and son."

"They're part of me," she said quietly. "Fighting the evil of cults is part of me, too, now."

"And it always will be. All of us are composites of our past experience. Our pasts shape us, make us who we are. But you can't change the past."

"I can give it meaning."

"You have."

"And where I wasn't able to save Matt and Aiden, I'm saving others. They didn't die in vain."

"I know. But you're not living, either, June. You're like an addict, obsessed with this fight, needing more and more, and if you don't stop, it's going to kill you. Even Rafe said so."

Anger mushroomed in her chest. "This is ridiculous," she said, trying to get up, but he held her back.

"Let me go, Jesse," she warned.

"You need balance," he countered, features stern, eyes unyielding. "And you need rest. Now."

"Who in hell are you to talk, anyway! Look at *you*—

haunted by your own demons for something you never even did, for closure you can't have."

Hurt flashed through his face and she hated herself even as the words came out of her mouth, but she was unable to stop.

"You couldn't even get that DNA test because then you'd have to face the truth."

His eyes narrowed.

"I learned something from losing my memory, June," he said very quietly, his voice thick. "For a short while I was forced to live entirely in the moment, and in that moment, I allowed myself to fall in love with you." He paused, his gaze tunneling into hers, intense. "I think you allowed yourself to drop into that moment with me. I think you do care. And I'm not going to let you throw this away now."

Her throat closed in on itself. Panic flared afresh. With it came a kind of pounding thrill, an undertow of exhilaration. He'd said he loved her.

Could she do it?

She glanced at the clock on the bedside table and tensed.

"Time is running out, Jesse. I can't think about the future now. I need to think about how to get Hannah and Michael out. I'm also due for a paramedic shift this afternoon. If I don't show, Samuel and Fargo are going to tie me with the missing henchmen. They're going to take a deeper look at Hannah. Something's going to give."

He swore softly. "You're like a pit bull on adrenaline, June. You *can't* even think anymore, can you? This is going to kill you, and you don't care, do you?"

June sucked in a chestful of air, and it hit her—Jesse was right, she hadn't cared. She knew she was on a one-way track until the end, and deep down in her subconscious maybe she wanted it to kill her. Because she had nothing else.

Now there was Jesse.

Now she *did* care.

She glanced slowly up into his eyes, and her heart wrenched at what she saw there. June bit her lip, struggling to hold down the huge painful and sudden surge of emotion burning in her chest. She reached down, felt Eager's velvet head, thought of wilderness and mountains and endless land. Tears pooled in her eyes. It was all she and Matt had ever dreamed of.

And now Jesse was offering it to her. He was offering her a second chance. He was trying to pull her back from the brink. And she was too scared to let him. He was right there, too. Because she was afraid to stop.

She was holding on to her guilt and her past as a way of escaping pain, as a way of fending off emotion, love. It was fear that was trapping her, not cults. Fear to feel—*really feel*—again. And she could see it now, through his eyes. Fear was at the root of it all—June Farrow, SAR worker, paramedic, so brave in the woods, so capable, so independent...and all she was, truly, deep down, was weak, alone. Afraid.

Jesse had cracked something in her open. And it was bleeding out.

"I promise," she said, very softly, "that I will rest after I've got Hannah out. Let me tie this job off, Jesse. If something happens to Hannah now, if I don't do something to help her now, I'll never be able to live with myself. I can get Michael out, too—he works with Hannah. She has a shift with him at the warehouse today." She paused. "*We* can get them both, Jesse. Help me do this one last thing, and I will help you honor your promise to Annie."

Emotion pooled in his eyes and twisted raw through his rugged features. He cupped her face, firmly, in his hands.

"Then will you at least just think about my proposal?"

"Yes," she whispered.

"I love you, June," he said, voice thick. And he kissed her, so tenderly, caringly, that she felt she was melting from the inside out, becoming fluid, one with him. And for a moment June wanted time to stand still, for him to hold her forever. She wanted, just for a while, to be cared for. To lean on him. And to be a team. It struck her then—she could have this. Possibly forever. If she was brave enough to reach out and take the hand he was offering to her.

While Jesse went to find some dry gear, June braided her hair in front of the mirror. Her arm was stiffening, and the pain was uncomfortable, but she knew her medicine and the wound wasn't going to kill her. She noted the deep black circles under her eyes, the contrasting pallor of her complexion. She'd lost weight, too—how had she not noticed that?

June realized with a start that she actually looked fragile, ill. Had she been so blind to herself as not to see? Had she been similarly blind to what was driving her into the ground?

She glanced down at the family photo of her, Matt, Aiden and their old yellow Lab, and a warmth filled June, an acceptance. She studied Matt's features, and Aiden's; the way they seemed so close, yet so independent; the way Matt had his arm over her shoulders. And June allowed all the good memories to come, to wash over her until she felt Eager nudge against her leg. Then she slipped off her wedding band, opened a small box on the dresser and removed a chain.

June slid the ring onto the chain and fastened it around her neck. The metal was warm on her skin. She clasped her hand over it.

Matt would want her to have a life. Maybe it really was time to move on—to let go of the bad memories, hold on to the good. To live in the present and dream of a future.

Samuel put down the phone after speaking to Mayor Rufus Kittridge. He leaned slowly back into his leather chair, trying to hold on to a measure of calm as he mulled over what Rufus had just told him.

Two of his henchmen, Lumpy Smithers and Harvey Daniels, had not returned after making apparent radio contact with Molly Rigg on the west flank where Lacy Matthews had vanished, and where the mystery mountain man had shot Jason Barnes.

Samuel chewed on several possible scenarios. The one that concerned him most was that Smithers and Daniels had fallen into the hands of Agent Hawk Bledsoe. Samuel knew how choked Lumpy was over the death of Jason Barnes. Lumpy could become a problem if offered a plea bargain by the feds. But in that event it would be Rufus who went down, not Samuel.

Still, if the good citizens of Cold Plains—his flock—learned that their kindly mayor was possibly a violent and dangerous man who killed any Devotees who attempted to escape, it was going to make things very complicated for Samuel. It could even signal the beginning of the end. Rage surged suddenly through him and he lurched to his feet and paced his office.

The more he'd thought about it, the more he'd begun to realize that vulnerable Devotees among his flock had first begun to "disappear" shortly after Mia Finn—Agent Bledsoe's new sister-in-law—had "defected" and apparently undergone deprogramming.

Samuel's thoughts turned again to the stranger in the woods who had helped Lacy escape.

Who was he?

His mind went to how June Farrow and her dog had found Lacy's kid's shoe on the opposite side of the mountain, miles away from where Smithers and Barnes had seen her fleeing in the dark. The image of June with that newcomer—Jesse

Marlboro—sifted into Samuel's mind. A cold, sinister suspicion began to unfurl in him.

He grabbed the phone on his desk and dialed Police Chief Bo Fargo.

"Fargo, when did June Farrow first arrive in town?"

"Early April, I think."

"When did the first Devotee disappear into a rumored safe-house program?"

Samuel could hear the sound of flicking paper—presumably Fargo looking something up.

"Actually, they started disappearing shortly after June Farrow's arrival in Cold Plains."

Samuel picked up a pencil, held it tight in his hand, his vision darkening. "She saw that paramedic job in the new paper—that's what brought her here?"

"Correct."

His hand fisted around the pencil. The old-fashioned clock on his paneled wall ticked. It was almost 9:00 a.m. "And you didn't notice these parallels before?"

Fargo cleared his throat. "June Farrow helped on the searches for the missing Devotees. There was no reason for mistrust."

Several beats of silence hung between them. Then Fargo said, "But recently, she has been acting out of character. She's been going over to Little Gulch for things she should be able to access here, like a vet, and then to pick up that Jesse Marlboro character she apparently used to date."

Rage peaked inside Samuel—he was surrounded by imbeciles.

"Check her out," he said very calmly. "See if her background story ties up. And take a deeper look at her landlady, Hannah Mendes. Also, look into the story behind this Jesse Marlboro, find out where Mia Finn went for deprogramming."

"You think June Farrow is part of the underground evacuation program?"

"That, Fargo, is your goddamn job!"

Samuel put the phone down and swore. Then he took a slow, deep breath—showing anger implied weakness. He must not display weakness. He was God to these people.

But the more Samuel considered it, the more it made sense for June Farrow to be the insider. The mole. The traitor. Stealing away members of his flock. The woman trying to personally undermine *him*.

A bitter and murderous rage blossomed through his chest. June Farrow was his enemy and he wanted her gone. Now.

Concern showed in Hannah Mendes's keen gray eyes as she opened her door to Jesse and June. "What's going on—what's happened?"

Jesse saw that Hannah's silver hair was long and tied smoothly back from a tanned and angular face. Even in her seventies Hannah was clearly an attractive woman with strong features and a slender body.

"We need to kill the evacuation program, Hannah," June said as she and Jesse entered Hannah's hallway.

"What do you mean?" Hannah said, pulling her sweater closer around her body.

"Two henchmen attacked the safe house last night. We had a mole inside, Molly Rigg. She led the attackers in via radio."

"Oh, my goodness." Hannah paled as her veined hand went to her chest. "Is everyone all right?"

"We're all fine—but things are going to blow. We need to pull you out, now."

"Come into the kitchen," Hannah said, leading the way. "I'm going to put the coffee on while you tell me everything."

"Agent Hawk Bledsoe and his team have Lumpy and Molly in custody, and it looks as though Hawk will soon be arresting Rufus Kittridge. He's apparently one of Samuel's lead henchmen, along with Monica Pearl."

"Are you serious?" Hannah hesitated, coffeepot in hand.

"Dead serious," June said, seating herself at the big wooden table in the middle of the warm and generously sized kitchen.

"I never pegged Rufus or Monica for being killers," Hannah said quietly. She put the pot on and took mugs from the cupboard. She moved with a certain elegance and grace, thought Jesse. And for a startling moment he could imagine June looking like Hannah at that age. The unbidden thought fueled the fire burning in him to have her with him forever. He glanced at June.

She caught his eyes in return. A moment passed between them. Hannah saw, and stilled briefly before busying herself with teaspoons and cream and sugar.

While Hannah poured the coffee, June told her who Jesse really was, and how he'd come to Cold Plains to free his brother-in-law.

"I know Mickey," Hannah said, seating herself across from them. "He's a dear boy—too vulnerable, too easily manipulated. I've been wanting to get him out for a while."

"Do you think we'll have a problem convincing him to leave, Hannah?" Jesse said.

Hannah pursed her lips. "He's not inclined to violence, if that's what you mean—not an angry bone in that boy's body. But he might be fearful and raise the alarm."

"I'll be ready to use force as an intervention if I have to," Jesse said. "But I don't want to. If you can help smooth my way with him, I'd be eternally grateful, Hannah."

Hannah nodded, glanced at June. "And you want to do this *today?*"

June leaned forward. "We *have* to move today, Hannah.

And we have to get you out today, as well. The evacuation program has become far too dangerous now."

"Oh, June, I can't just leave. There will still be people who need me, who need to escape Samuel, *especially* if things start to go off the rails now that Hawk is closing in."

"Hannah, you're not going to help anyone dead."

She set her mug slowly onto the table. "I don't run, June." She shot Jesse a glance, a hint of reproach in her keen gray eyes, as if he was somehow responsible for the decision to kill the evacuation program. As if he'd swayed June in some way. "Nor do you run, June," she said.

"I do, Hannah," June said quietly. "I've been running a long time." June reached for Jesse's hand and covered it with her own as she caught his eyes. "It's time I stopped running now and faced my fears. Faced change."

His heart almost burst.

"Besides, Hawk and his FBI team *are* closing in. It's not going to be long now and this *will* be over."

Hannah shook her head, her eyes sad. "My heart is in these mountains, June, in this valley. I grew up on this ranch. I buried my husband here. I cannot just up and leave. Where would I go?"

"The cave house is still safe, for now," June said.

"And for how long, if what you say is true? And I'm not as confident as you that Samuel is going down without a very long fight, yet. Where would I go in the interim? I have no-where."

"My place." The words came out of Jesse's mouth before he even thought them through.

June and Hannah both looked at him.

He cleared his throat. "I have a ranch in the Wind River foothills, Hannah. You'll love it—all the mountains and space you could ever need. I've got guest cottages, horses. You could stay there for as long as it takes for the feds to wind things up with Samuel here."

Hannah stared at him. And June's eyes said it all—*thank you*. The affection he felt coming from her made his heart swell.

"Do it, Hannah," June said, leaning forward. "Go pack a bag with the essentials, now. Give it to Jesse. He'll keep it with him in my truck after he's dropped me off at the Urgent Care Center for my ambulance shift later today, then he'll immediately drive out and park near the warehouse. You go to work as normal. Then at about 3:30 p.m., shortly after I've started my shift, you get yourself near Michael and a telephone, and you develop serious chest pains."

"I don't know, June, that's like tempting the fates. I don't like to tempt the fates."

"It's about getting yourself and Michael to safety, Hannah. Samuel's deception must be fought with deception of its own. It's what we do, remember?"

Hannah inhaled deeply. "What then?"

"You ask Michael to call 9-1-1. Dispatch will send the call straight through to me. The dispatcher will keep Michael on the line, near you, which is what we want. I'll bring the ambulance around to the warehouse door at the back."

"Aren't there two of you in the ambulance?" Hannah said.

June nodded. "Ted is on call with me this afternoon. He'll be driving. The whole thing will seem very real to him, Hannah, given your age. No offense."

"None taken." Hannah smiled. "I think."

"Chest pains are funny things," June said. "Not to be taken lightly even if there is no other physical sign of distress, so I'll get out the gurney, insist you come to the hospital for a checkup. You hang on to Michael's hand, tell him you need him to come in the ambulance for moral support."

"That could work," said Hannah. "Mickey would bend

over backward to help anyone, and he does have a soft spot for me—we've built a bond."

"So he'll trust you. That's good. Meanwhile, Jesse will be waiting outside the building with my truck, parked right near the delivery entrance where we'll back the ambulance up. If anyone asks, he'll say he's come to pick up a check from you for ranch supplies."

Hannah nodded. "That would ring true, since he's my new hired help."

"Good. Then while Ted and I push you on the gurney back to the waiting ambulance, you start fretting about your purse and the money inside, or whatever. Make a scene. I'll tell Ted to go back and get your purse. While he does, Jesse grabs Michael, and I get you off that gurney, stat, and into the waiting truck. If all goes to plan, we'll be gone before Ted even returns, especially if you put your purse in a place difficult to find."

Hannah stared at them. Silence swelled, and the kitchen clock ticked.

"This is really it?" Hannah said quietly.

"It's down to the wire now, Hannah."

"We can never come back after we pull something like this off—not while Samuel is still around."

June nodded.

"Are you *sure* it's that dire?"

"Even Hawk Bledsoe said this whole place is set to blow," Jesse said. "No one wants another Waco, but Samuel is apparently getting desperate, and who knows how far he will go to protect what he has?"

Hannah sucked in a deep breath. "Okay…let's do it."

Chapter 12

June's heart pounded as they burst out of the warehouse pushing Hannah on the gurney toward the waiting ambulance, Michael running at their side as he held on to Hannah's hand.

Jesse stepped out of the shadows behind the warehouse door. "Michael!" he whispered.

Michael froze dead in his tracks at the sudden sight of his brother-in-law, shock, confusion, then fear crossing his face.

"Quick, Michael, over here," Jesse said in a harsh whisper.

"Jesse? What...what are you doing here? Is Annie here?"

"I need to talk to you about Annie, Michael—"

"My purse!" Hannah suddenly screamed hysterically. "I left my purse inside. I need it. It has my money, medication, everything in it!"

Ted shot a glance at June.

"I—I've got to have my purse!"

"Ted, can you go back and get it for her?" June leaned

down and said calmly to Hannah, "Where is it? Can you tell him?"

"It's…by my desk in the accounting office at the back of the warehouse."

"Go," June said briskly to Ted. "I'll be fine getting her in by myself. We'll be ready to roll as soon as you're back."

He hesitated. "Go!" insisted June forcefully. "We might need whatever medication she has in there."

Relief washed through her as Ted turned and raced back into the building.

"Quick." She rapidly unstrapped Hannah and helped her off the stretcher. Taking her arm, they rushed toward the idling truck before Ted could return. To June's shock Michael was sitting passively in the backseat with Jesse behind the wheel.

June helped Hannah into the back so she could sit beside Michael and keep him calm. She flung herself into the passenger seat, slammed the door. "Go!"

Jesse hit the gas and wheeled out of the warehouse parking lot, tires spinning on loose gravel. He headed for the road that would take them to Little Gulch.

June turned around in her seat. Michael was crying softly in the back, murmuring Annie's name. Hannah's hand rested on his knee.

"I told him about Annie," Jesse said, eyes fixed on the road as they sped past the ranches, heading toward the mountains. The plan was to drive straight out to Little Gulch and leave Hannah there with her sister-in-law while a flight out to Wind River could be organized for her.

June, Jesse and Michael would meanwhile tackle the long hike back to the cave house from Little Gulch. The hike would be too much for Hannah, and there was no point in bringing her unnecessarily all the way back to the safe house.

Jesse had contacted his ranch manager, who would send a vehicle to welcome Hannah at the airstrip in Wind River.

"He didn't know about Annie and the fire?" June said.

"No. I told him briefly what happened, and that I'd promised Annie I'd come get him. It was all such a shock he came peaceably."

"It's going to be okay, Michael," June said softly, turning around in her seat to hand him some tissues.

Michael's face was still as open and innocent as a young boy's, his eyes large and filled with pain. Her heart went out to him. "I promise you it's going to be all right."

"I—I didn't know," Michael sobbed. "I would've come if I'd known about the fire, if Jesse could have gotten hold of me—"

"We didn't have a contact number, Michael," said Jesse.

"S-Samuel t-told me it would be better not to have any contact until…I got a solid grasp on being the best me I could be. S-Samuel said family often tries to stop you from im-provement. They're the gatekeepers, he said. They t-try to sabotage you." He blew his nose. "I feel so bad, Jesse. I wasn't even there for her memorial service."

"There's nothing you could have done, Michael," Jesse said, eyes still on the road, his shoulders tight. "I'll tell you more about what happened when we get somewhere safe, but Annie made me vow to come find you, and I did. She wanted you safe. She understood what was happening here. And she will now rest in peace because you're out of there."

"You did the right thing, Mickey," Hannah said gently, putting her arm around the young man. "You'll see. June's right—it's all going to be okay."

They drove in silence, the ribbon of road undulating behind them as they left Cold Plains in the distance. Up ahead, along the distant horizon, there was a break in the cloud and sun streamed through onto the mountains.

June reached out and placed her hand on Jesse's knee.

"Thank you," she said quietly. "We make a good team."

He shot her a glance, unable to temper the light in his eyes, and a ghost of a smile curved his lips. "That's what I kept trying to tell you," he said.

Jesse took one hand off the wheel, covered hers on his knee and realized the wedding band on her finger was gone.

He felt a lump form in his throat, and emotion pricked behind his eyes. And he knew he'd won. He was going to take her home.

Five days later...

News of Mayor Rufus Kittridge's arrest by the FBI spread like wildfire through town as Devotees flocked down to the municipal offices to watch in shock and horror as their avuncular mayor was handcuffed and frog-marched by agents in bulletproof vests toward a waiting federal vehicle.

Samuel watched the whole thing from his window—the feds taking *his* mayor, his key militia leaders. His ace in the hole. Rage pounded through his blood—the effrontery of it, right there in the street below his own office window.

He stilled suddenly as he saw another two federal agents marching Monica Pearl down the street toward the gleaming black SUVs. Monica wore a summer dress of modest length, patterned with small roses—Samuel knew the dress intimately. Her blond hair was tied back demurely and her pretty cheeks were flushed—he could see that even from here.

People were gathering on sidewalks to watch, many of them Devotees who'd arrived early for the nightly seminar. And right then, as the bumbling agents put the handcuffed

Monica into the black SUV and closed the door on her, the bells of the community center began to peal—calling his Devotees to the seminar.

Hawk Bledsoe had orchestrated the whole thing for maximum effect, to undermine Samuel in the eyes of his Devotees. Before Hawk got into his own vehicle, he glanced up at Samuel's window, catching his eyes.

It was like a punch to his gut.

The shameless, impudent boldness of it! The barefaced audacity—parading Rufus and Monica in front of the others like that, staging a production designed to undermine *him,* Samuel Grayson! It cut to the heart of his pride, his grasp on complete power. Now he was going to be forced to address this incident in his seminar tonight, and it was going to look as if he was covering something up.

A knock sounded on his oak door.

He swung around.

It was his assistant, Jenny Smith. "I started the bells ringing, Samuel. You will be at your seminar tonight, won't you?"

"Why the hell not!" he barked, his face feeling hot. He hated that. He never showed loss of control in front of a loyal Devotee.

He breathed in deep and then exhaled slowly, counting to three. He smiled warmly.

"I apologize, Jenny. The arrest of Mayor Kittridge has come as a big surprise to us all—I'm still personally reeling from the shock, but the seminar will go on as planned."

"They say he's going to be charged with murder, of our *own,*" she whispered. "I even heard rumors he could be involved in the Cold Plains Five murders, and Monica Pearl, too… I just can't believe—"

"And so you shouldn't," said Samuel. "The FBI needs to show something for their efforts here, and this is simply a witch hunt." Samuel placed his hand on Jenny's shoulder.

"In fact, it's a sign we're finally achieving our goals. Because the higher you go, Jenny," he said affectionately, "the better you become, the more it threatens people who have not managed to improve their own lives." His gaze held hers so she couldn't escape, couldn't think, couldn't do anything other than look at him, hear the authoritative but kind cadence of his voice, see the wisdom in his eyes.

"You *know* you are successful when people like Agent Hawk Bledsoe move in like parasites. They will try to tear down what we have built, and, more than ever now, we must rally together during this trial."

Jenny smiled, nodded. "Thank you, Samuel."

The adoration in her eyes bolstered him.

"Now go. And, Jenny," Samuel called out behind her, "make sure the bell rings extra loud and extra long tonight. I shall be holding a very special address."

Samuel listened as the peals designed to resemble an old church bell—sonorous and uplifting and goose-bump inducing—resounded down the streets of Cold Plains, Wyoming, through his cleaned-up cowboy town, across the ranches and into the hills and forests where somewhere there was rumored to be a safe house he had yet to find.

And outside, down in the streets, the doors of the black federal vehicles closed, and they drove off in a convoy with flashing lights as they took away Mayor Rufus Kittridge and Monica Pearl.

June came out of the room where she'd been counseling Michael.

"How's he doing?" Jesse said.

She smiled. "Great. He's a good kid, Jesse. He's totally guileless and so easily manipulated, but the shock of actually seeing you in Cold Plains, and hearing about his older sister's death at the same time, jolted him right out of whatever spell Samuel had him under. He's going to be fine."

He touched her arm. "Come outside. I've got sundowners out on the patio."

The cave house was empty at the moment, apart from her, Jesse, Michael and Eager. Over the past five days June and Jesse had moved the others out to where they could access further counseling from EXIT and go on to new lives.

"Michael needs a dog," June said as she followed Jesse out onto the stone patio. "He's thriving in the company of Eager—" She stilled suddenly at the sight before her.

The sky was streaked with cirrus clouds that had been painted hot-pink and orange by the sinking sun. The air was warm and filled with the soft sound of birds.

Jesse grinned. "See? I thought it might be nice to sit out here for a bit."

Her heart filled. She loved him more than she could imagine. But as she moved toward the stone table, she froze again, this time at a sound in the distance.

"Did you hear that?"

Jesse came up beside her and listened, the warm evening breeze ruffling his hair.

"It's Samuel's bells," he said.

She nodded. "Sometimes when the air currents are just right you can hear them ringing all the way over here, summoning his flock to the community center."

"You think he's worried?"

"He has to be," said June. "Hawk was going to do the arrests right before the seminar." She looked at her watch. "If all went to plan, Rufus Kittridge and Monica Pearl should be in federal custody about now, thanks to the quick plea-bargain acceptance from both Lumpy Smithers and Molly Rigg."

"You've done good here, June."

"I'm not done yet. Samuel still has to go down."

"It'll happen. Soon." He put his arm around her shoulders and drew her close as they stood watching the clouds change color and the sky deepen to indigo—the same color as Jesse's eyes, thought June. His eyes were the color of an early-evening sky. Up high above the forest, two eagles soared, watchful over the Wyoming hills and valleys.

"Mostly," he said, very quietly, "I want to thank you for saving my life, June, and for helping me honor my vow to Annie. I can move forward now."

"Did you love her, Jesse?"

He was silent for a long while.

"I stopped being able to love Annie some time ago," he said quietly. "Maybe we weren't even a good match to start with, but I like to believe we could have made a go of it, because when I make a promise, June, the commitment, it's everything to me."

"I know," she whispered as she leaned into him, enjoying the solid strength of his body, the fact she actually had someone to lean on after all these years.

"We could be good together, you know that?" he said.

She smiled. "Yeah," she said softly, "I think we could."

Jesse's heart kicked. *Easy, boy—don't rush it. You came on way too fast and strong the other night, asking her to move in with you so soon.*

He said cautiously, "June, once our work here—"

She glanced up at him. "*Our* work?"

"Which part did you miss about being a team?"

"Yes, but—"

"But what? I want to help you finish here. You helped me put my promise to Annie to bed, now I want to help you fulfill your promise to Matt and Aiden."

She stared at him. "It was never like that, Jesse—it wasn't a promise."

"Well," he said, a mischievous playfulness entering his rugged features, "I wasn't going to call it an obsession or anything."

She laughed, and, damn, it felt good to be able to laugh about something like that. Then she sobered as she saw lust darkening in his eyes.

"I'm not scared to let them go anymore." She smiled. "I'm not afraid to take a second chance." She leaned up, hooking her arms around his neck, drawing him down to her.

"I love you, Jesse Marlboro," she whispered against his lips.

He smiled against her mouth. "Grainger."

She shook her head. "I always wanted a mountain cowboy, just like in those old ads, so I'm going to keep my Marlboro Man." And she kissed him as the sun began to sink behind the hills, and the bells in Cold Plains grew silent.

Three days later...

The FBI had made further arrests and laid charges against Rufus Kittridge and Monica Pearl for their roles in three of the Cold Plains Five murders, specifically twenty-nine-year-old Shelby Jackson, thirty-four-year-old Laurel Pierce and twenty-five-year-old Abby Michaels.

Shelby Jackson was rumored to have been dating Samuel Grayson when she'd disappeared five years ago. Laurel Pierce was the estranged wife of local rancher Nathan Pierce. And Abby Michaels was the mother of Rafe Black's still-missing nine-month-old son, Devin.

Agent Hawk Bledsoe had informed June and Jesse that he expected to get more evidence soon, something to finally nail Samuel himself. But until then, everyone remained restless and nervous—things were coming to a head.

Meanwhile, June and Jesse had driven out from Little

Gulch to meet Darcy Craven two towns over. From there they'd hiked in to where the body of Jane Doe, murder victim number two, had been found.

Darcy now stood atop a rocky ridge, hands on her hips as she caught her breath. Her cheeks were pink from exertion and her hair damp from a soft summer rain. All around them the forest was shrouded in heavy layers of mist.

They'd been following Eager on an air-scent search all morning, and they'd found nothing apart from litter and the odd garment left by hikers.

While Darcy rested and June watered Eager, Jesse had gone down the opposite side of the ridge to check out a small trail they'd seen earlier.

"June, I want to thank you both for doing this," Darcy said. "I know you didn't believe we'd find anything. But I just had to come and look."

"Hey, it's the least we could do, Darcy. I just wish we *could* find something for you that would help with your mother's identity," June said as she screwed the cap back onto her water bottle.

"Isn't this near where Samuel once had a cabin?" Darcy asked, turning in a full circle.

"I had no idea he had a cabin in these parts," said June, checking her GPS.

Darcy frowned and bit the inside of her cheek. "I *think* the cabin was supposed to be in this area—I'm sure that's what I heard Officer Ford say some time ago, that Samuel and his brother used to camp out this way when they were young."

June reached for her radio and keyed it. "June for Jesse?" she released the key and the radio crackled.

"At your service, K9 team."

June grinned, and keyed again. "Any signs of an old cabin down your way?"

"Negative. Trail seems to go nowhere. I'm going to head back up."

But as June hooked the radio onto her belt, Eager's hackles rose and his tail suddenly went straight as an arrow. June stilled, feeling a sudden eeriness, as if they were being watched.

"Easy, boy," she whispered to Eager as she turned in a slow circle, carefully scanning the woods, her hand going instinctively for her weapon.

"What is it?" Darcy came up to her side, suddenly nervous.

"Are you sure you weren't followed out here, Darcy?"

"I—I'm pretty sure."

A branch cracked. June spun to face the trees from whence the noise had come. She waited.

Fingers of mist curled out from the trees, swirling around the bases like wraiths. Branches rustled suddenly. June's mouth went bone-dry.

Eager growled, baring fangs.

"Who's there?" June called as she drew her gun and clicked off the safety.

"Maybe it's an animal," whispered Darcy.

"It's human," June said, eyes fixed on the bushes. "Eager reacts differently for animals."

A dark shape moved suddenly behind the branches.

"Identify yourself or I'll shoot!" June yelled.

Silent as the swirling mist, a dark shape shifted forward. June's heart began to thud. It was a man. Tall, broad of shoulder. Wearing military-style camouflage gear. And as he emerged from the mist she saw he held a shotgun. It was aimed right at her face.

"It's *Samuel!*" Darcy hissed, grabbing June's arm.

Sweat broke out over June's body. He came closer, his eyes transfixed by Darcy. "My God," he said to Darcy. "You look just like Catherine."

Darcy slumped to the ground in a dead faint. And up close, June saw that while this man was almost the spitting image of Samuel Grayson, he was not the cult leader.

"My name is Micah," the man said, lowering his weapon and crouching down beside Darcy, feeling for her pulse. She came around as Micah touched her, and he helped her into a sitting position, staring hard at her.

"You really do look like Catherine George—we used to come out here to the cabin. Her, me, Samuel. Sometimes others."

June swallowed as it hit her square between the eyes—she was looking at Samuel Grayson's fraternal twin, the legendary mercenary. The man Hawk Bledsoe had been searching for to help him take Samuel down.

Micah turned his attention to June. His features were fiercely handsome, his hair dark, his eyes a vivid green, and he exuded the same palpable presence that his powerful brother did—except different.

"I'm June Farrow," she said, still a little unsure of whether to holster her Glock. To her relief she saw Jesse coming up the ridge. And before Micah could aim his twelve-gauge at Jesse, June said, "And that's Jesse Grainger."

Jesse froze for a nanosecond.

"It's not Samuel," June called out to him. "It's his twin, Micah Grayson."

They all stared at him, a little in awe. The Mercenary had returned.

* * * * *

SUSPENSE

Harlequin® ROMANTIC SUSPENSE

COMING NEXT MONTH
AVAILABLE MAY 29, 2012

REQUEST YOUR FREE BOOKS!
2 FREE NOVELS PLUS 2 FREE GIFTS!

ROMANTIC
SUSPENSE

Sparked by Danger, Fueled by Passion.

*Harlequin® Romantic Suspense presents the final book
in the gripping* PERFECT, WYOMING *miniseries
from best-loved veteran series author Carla Cassidy*

*Witness as mercenary Micah Grayson and cult escapee
Olivia Conner join forces to save a little boy and to take
down a monster, while desire explodes between them....*

Read on for an excerpt from
MERCENARY'S PERFECT MISSION

Available June 2012 from Harlequin® Romantic Suspense.

"**I** won't tell," she exclaimed fervently. "Please don't hurt
me. I swear I won't tell anyone what I saw. Just let me have
my other son and we'll go far away from here. I'll never
speak your name again." Her voice cracked as she focused
on his gun and he realized she believed he was Samuel.

Certainly it was dark enough that it would be easy for
anyone to mistake him for his brother. When the brothers
were together it was easy to see the subtle differences
between them. Micah's face was slightly thinner, his
features more chiseled than those of his brother.

At the moment Micah knew Samuel kept his hair cut
neat and tidy, while Micah's long hair was tied back. He
reached up and pulled the rawhide strip, allowing his hair
to fall from its binding.

The woman gasped once again. "You aren't him...but
you look like him. Who are you?" Her voice still held fear
as she dropped the stick and protectively clutched the baby
closer to her chest.

"Who are you?" he countered. He wasn't about to be
taken in by a pale-haired angel with big green eyes in this
evil place where angels probably couldn't exist.

HRSEXP0612

"I'm Olivia Conner, and this is my son Sam." Tears filled her eyes. "I have another son, but he's still in town. I couldn't get to him before I ran away. I've heard rumors that there was a safe house somewhere, but I've been in the woods for two days and I can't find it."

Micah was unmoved by her tears and by her story. He knew how devious his brother could be, and Micah would do everything possible to protect the location of the safe house. There was only one way to know for sure if she was one of Samuel's "devotees."

Will Olivia be able to get her son back from the clutches of evil? Or will Micah's maniacal twin put an end to them all? Find out in the shocking conclusion to the PERFECT, WYOMING *miniseries.*

MERCENARY'S PERFECT MISSION
Available June 2012, only from
Harlequin® Romantic Suspense, wherever books are sold.

Harlequin®

SPECIAL EDITION

Life, Love and Family

USA TODAY bestselling author

Marie Ferrarella

enchants readers in

ONCE UPON A MATCHMAKER

Micah Muldare's aunt is worried that her nephew is going to wind up alone in his old age…but this matchmaking mama has just the thing! When Micah finds himself accused of theft, defense lawyer Tracy Ryan agrees to help him as a favor to his aunt, but soon finds herself drawn to more than just his case. Will Micah open up his heart and realize Tracy is his match?

Available June 2012

Saddle up with Harlequin® series books this summer and find a cowboy for every mood!

Available wherever books are sold.

www.Harlequin.com

HSE65674